A Wicked Wa...

I gave him a hearty shake for good measure and he whimpered, "Let me be, Mr. Sturrock, I want no part of it," while at that same instant Maggsy screeched louder still and dragged me sideways with a jolt. That instant also something flew shining between Moses and me and hung quivering in the woodwork, as for one more instant we sat gazing at it with the din continuing unabated, the wench screaming "Rape!" and Maggsy whispering, "Sweet Jesus, that near enough filleted you." It was a heavy-bladed throwing knife buried three inches deep in the wood, and had it struck either of us would have split his head or mine like an apple. Moses gave vent to a sound like an expiring pig and slipped off the bench and under the table, but I am made of sterner stuff; and was moreover enraged.

Other titles in the Walker British Mystery series:

A WICKED
WAY TO DIE

J.G.
Jeffreys

WALKER AND COMPANY · NEW YORK

First published in the United States of America in 1973 by the
Walker Publishing Company, Inc.

This paperback edition first published in 1983.

ISBN: 0-8027-3032-9

Library of Congress Catalog Card Number: 73-83194

Printed in the United States of America

10 9 8 7 6 5 4 3 2 1

CHAPTER ONE

I am advised by others of this miserable tribe of penny pinched scribblers that for the benefit of such unfortunates as have not yet perused my late work* I should give some fresh account of myself and that most horrible, lecherous and bloodthirsty little rogue Maggsy, my clerk. Nor am I unwilling, for I know of no subject which gives me greater pleasure than myself; my desperate adventures with all manner of villains and cut throats, my confounding them by a philosophical application of the Art and Science of Detection, and the moral observations which I let fall freely now and again to the general great improvement.

In short I am a most proper man. Merry in bed with a deserving wench, but of a particular gentility with the nobility and gentry and especially with the ladies; of benevolent manner except when in choler, and a generosity which sometimes gets the better of me, yet a terror to sinners and uncommonly handy with my fists or my pistols when needs must. So there you have me; Jeremy Sturrock of the Bow Street Runners in our year of 1800 and risen to my present eminence, even as one of the personal bodyguards to His Majesty King George III, God bless him, from most humble beginnings; my old father being no

---

*The Thieftaker, which may still be obtained from my booksellers; being an ingenious and diverting tale which alone is worth the modest cost, not counting instruction in the Art and Science of Detection and numerous moral observations included gratis, thus rendering a work of treble value for the money.

more than a coster-monger, poor simple soul. It was from the streets of London that I learned my observation of human nature, my letters from an ancient screever and my learning from a drunken old lawyer's clerk—he died of a flux of gin in the end—but my wits came straight from Providence Himself; to the end, I am persuaded, of confounding villainy and bettering many a rascal by a good hanging.

As for this Maggsy, he is a kind of urchin which I picked up in my kindness while about that business of the Village of Rogues, where he was begging and starving at the King's Head Inn. A chimney sweeper's boy run away from his master, of mean and bony stature, some twelve to fourteen years—not being quite clear of that himself but more than old enough in wickedness—and a little monster of singular ugliness, with blood and disaster for his chief delights. Out of my natural tenderness I took up the creature to save him from his natural end, and also to provide myself at small cost with a boot boy, servant, footman, messenger and clerk in my lodging at Soho Square, London, above Mrs Spilsbury's Dispensary; the said Mrs Spilsbury being an elegant consultant in matters of the gout, fluxes, humours, the pox, debility in bed and suchlike.

Maggsy is an indifferent poor clerk, but I persevere with the toad and have him taught his letters by an old canonical screever whom I keep out of Newgate Prison for my own purposes; these chiefly to keep me informed on all that passes in the stews of Seven Dials insofar as mortal man can know this—as even Providence, Who will observe a sparrow fall, is here inclined to hold His Nose and look the other way. Being a fallen parson our Holy Moses passes for a learned man when he is not steeped in gin, which is about every third Thursday and sometimes on Sunday when he has a fit of the remorses. To be plain he is a snivelling rogue, but being a screever—which for the information of the genteel is a writer of begging letters, conning de-

clarations, false testimonials and other criminal epistles—
he has a command of our noble English language which is
little less than that of the late and lamented Doctor Samuel
Johnson himself. Moreover he is heavy with a back hander
when he can aim straight, which is the one sure way of
hammering instruction into the young and in especial
Master Maggsy.

So for our present light and diverting reminiscence and
singular mystery you are to observe me this night of
October in the pit of the Theatre Royal, Drury Lane,
attending the play and contemplating the animated scene.
You shall observe a blaze of innumerable candles about
the boxes and circles up to the dark and elevated perch of
the Gods, these sparkling alike on villain and virtuous,
beaux, bucks and dandies by their own reckoning the
flower and wit of London, some few ladies and more
whores. A mirror of fashion and the mode; chemise gowns
like pretty flowers though few so innocent, and some even
attired in that lewd and indecent Frenchy style of the
Directory. Ladies, I beseech you, when you fling away
modesty what have you left but goose pimples?

The play was a poor slight thing of no great weight and
little like to restore Mr Sheridan's fortunes, but well enough
received and the Gods not throwing much above a few
orange peels and nut shells at the players. This followed
by a Grand Patriotic Spectacle to celebrate our recent vic-
tories at sea and described 'Britannia Subduing the Waves';
Britannia being a certain Mrs Huxey attended by her train
of Nymphs, Sea Monsters and Bold British Tars. A notable
figure of a woman, and could she be brought only to fall
upon that little Corsican tyrant Bonaparte she'd squash
the rogue flat and we should have no more trouble of him.
Waving her trident, damned near putting out the eye of
one of her nymphs with it and close enough spitting a
sailor, she cried 'Then subside at my command, ye raging
billows, begone ye monsters of the deep', this noble senti-

ment then saluted by such a belch of cannon, banging of drums, flashes of lightning and fanfares of trumpets the like you never heard before.

As you shall see that uproar had a great part of what followed, though at this instant I had no thought but the shouts of 'Huzza', the ladies screaming and swooning into their beaux' arms to be revived with glasses of wine, the commoner sort of the Gods roaring and hallooing, and one gallant so beside himself with patriotic fervour as to fling a bottle of claret on the stage; an ungenteel act as it might well have killed a sailor. But at length peace is restored and the billows stilled—an effect made by small boys, in some danger of suffocation, rolling and tossing under a cloth laid over the boards—while Britannia receives the homage of her Nymphs, the retreat of the Sea Monsters and the support of her Bold British Tars. Upon which she descends from her throne, advances to the footlamps like a ship of war herself, and declaims, 'Thus will I quell, thus rule this yeasty main; far flung from our great island's shores, for distant climes to gain', to the end of another tumult of cheers, yells, catcalls and orange peels. A most improving spectacle.

It was in the midst of this final clamour that I felt a plucking at my elbow, and turned to perceive Master Maggsy whispering at me with a face which I knew well could only mean disaster and devilment. Thinking to improve the little monster's mind, if such a miracle were possible, I had brought him to the theatre with me but the rogue had slipped away half an hour since, no doubt about some mischief of his own; and by the look of him now he had amply discovered it. 'You'd best come quick,' he announced, 'there's blood atrickling under the door.'

'Where have you been, you jackanapes?' I demanded. 'And what blood?'

'Dunno what blood,' he answered, 'but there's a stink of gunpowder with it, and the door locked but they're settling

8

to break it down and I'm off to see what's doing, I ain't agoing to miss that. You'd best come; there's a deader for sure.'

'What?' I started again, but the rogue was gone, thrusting his way through the press as they saluted our Britannia with patriotic fervour, that noble figure now with some miss-tossed orange impaled upon her trident. I had no choice but to follow the rogue, and to confess the truth my own curiosity was whetted, for Master Maggsy has a natural nose for calamity. It is my belief that when this child falls into Hell, a mercy of Providence which cannot now be long delayed, he will find his way about the sulphurous Pit before Satan himself knows he's there; and indeed, when he led me through a little trap beside the fiddler's pit, the under stage at the Lane was not unlike Hell, such an ill lit gloom and stink, such a shadowy tangle of contrivances and pulleys, and such a confused roaring, creaking and groaning from above, with Maggsy scurrying through it like a minor devil himself and whispering, 'I'm afeared they'll have it open by now.'

So at last we came to a passage, with candles guttering in wall sconces, a row of doors to each side not unlike prison cells, and a knot of people clustered about one, chattering and peering. I noted a front house flunkey, his wig awry, two or three of the actors from the play somewhat unbuttoned, a gentleman of the better sort and one or two stage mechanics, etc.; also Mother Knapp the fruit woman, with her pannier of oranges and nuts. This last being also of certain other trades in the sins of Drury Lane; to be short a most notorious female pander and whoremonger. They fell back at my presence, and Maggsy jerked his thumb down at a thin red trickle creeping out from beneath the door. It looked near enough like blood in the candlelight and I demanded, 'What have we here?'

Mother Knapp let out a screech on a great gust of porter. 'God ha' mercy, 'tis Sturrock the thieftaker; a fearful man.

9

And here we've death and murder.'

Bending down to examine this appearance closer, the light not being all that good, I put my finger to it; and if that were blood it was uncommon thin. I announced, 'Why now, your sight's failing or you need better candles. That's mere burgundy or claret.'

'Begod, is it so?' one of the actors asked, a pert coxcomb. 'Here we've a smart rogue, this thieftaker.'

I was about to make him a short answer when the more gentlemanly fellow stayed me, saying, 'No, Jack; you take it too light. There's something amiss here for certain.'

' 'Tis Mr Robert Mytton,' the flunkey offered, eyeing me sideways, 'in there and the door locked, nor he don't answer. And I'll swear there was a stink of gunpowder about afore the draught blowed it away. This place is too draughty for hell.'

'If that's Bob Mytton,' the coxcomb observed, 'and he don't come to the door it's more like there's another virgin gone, for that's the ladies' common dressing chamber. That is,' he added on an afterthought, 'if there ever was a virgin in this theatre.'

'Your impudence is out of place, sir,' I reproved him and commanded the flunkey, 'Have that door open, my man. Put your shoulder against it.'

By now Master Maggsy had his eye clapped to the keyhole, which was one of that sort commonly closed with a little flap or plate of brass, and he announced, 'Ain't nothing to be seen; it's blocked t'other side, and it's fast right enough.'

The flunkey hung back muttering something of taking his orders from Mr Knyvet, the House Manager, and in no mood for further discussion, sweeping him and Maggsy aside, I lifted my foot and applied the heel of it to the lock in no gentle manner. I cannot put up with being crossed by the lower orders, and as I was passing impatient by now the door flew open with a crash to reveal such a scene as any honest man would wish never to view again. For a space while you might have counted five we all stood gazing on the awful spectacle, before Mother Knapp screeched, 'God Christ', and swooned clean away, falling into the flunkey's arms with all her oranges bouncing everywhere; while even Maggsy for all his ghoulish humour could only whisper, 'God's Tripes, I never see a mess like that before.'

I advanced delicately, sniffing at the reek of paint and perfume and gunpowder, the stink of candles and blood. For your better understanding of what follows I shall particularise on the chamber, this being a middling sized place with but one small window high up under the ceiling and that, again like a Newgate cell, so close barred that not even a cat could have entered through it. Along one wall was a kind of bench with a number of looking glasses and candles and a litter of pots and jars; several chairs with articles of feminine attire cast about them, and shawls and bonnets and such like tossed on an old day bed with the stuffing coming out. At one end a row of female garments hanging against the wall, at the other a small guarded fireplace with a sulky fire of sea coal and, you shall note, only the one door; this pushed back as I had flung it open, and lying by it that which had given the appearance of blood; a claret bottle rolling on its side and still with some remains of wine in it.

But the most piteous and awful part was cast upon the bare boards away from the bench. A youngish fellow, not above five or six and twenty by the look of him, lying on his back with an up-tipped chair slewed away from him and a short barrelled pistol close by his right hand, the forefinger indeed still resting loosely on its trigger. Save for a little blackening about his lips the face was near enough unscathed; but beyond that I will leave it to the tender minded to fancy what a charge of powder and ball will do to the back of a man's skull if he place a pistol

11

muzzle in his mouth and discharge it. With Maggsy beside me feasting his ghoulish eyes I stood gazing down at the sad remains, and in particular contemplating that finger on the trigger. I will say simply now that it was a wicked way to die.

At last I turned to face the crowd whispering and shoving there, some of them by the door now thrust back against the wall, and all variously affected. Even that coxcomb actor was a long shot less pleased with himself, though he strove to put an impudent face on it, muttering, 'God's Teeth, he made a most damnable hash of himself.'

I looked at him hard and asked, 'Your name, sir?' upon which he pointed his knee, announcing, 'Jack Dashwood, sir; your obedient servant,' while I restrained a desire to teach him better manners in the presence of the dead and myself. But giving him another look which should have quelled him I turned my attention to the other.

This was of a somewhat different sort; plumper, softer, a face somewhat like a baby's arse, with sandy fair hair, very likely the simpleton of the piece by the cut of him, but now with a greenish colour about his chaps. Shaking a bit and stuttering he got out, 'Nicholas Lilley'.

The gentlemanly fellow and, as I have already observed, seemingly not of the Thespian brotherhood—for you shall note that no more than any poor scribbler does an actor rise to join the gentry until he becomes famous—announced himself plain and straightforward. 'Tom Cullen. But is it of any matter, sir? Should we not do something for poor Bob here?'

'There's little can be done,' I answered, 'save by the coroner's officers. Do I have him aright? One Bob or Robert Mytton?'

'The younger,' he agreed. 'Of Mytton and Company, the bankers. And a rare good fellow. Who'd ha' thought he'd do that to himself?'

'There's a tale that he's at odds with the old man,' the

actor Lilley chimed in. 'It's said old Mytton threatens to lodge a guinea in the bank and let him live on the interest. But, be damned, he'd only to lift his finger to marry a fortune.' He cast a sidelong glance at the other one, Dashwood.

'He done it for love,' Mother Knapp screeched, now on her knees peering between the legs of the two mechanics, the while scrabbling about to gather up her fallen oranges and her own two saddle bag tits like to fall out of her bodice and join the said fruits on the floor. 'All for love of little Mistress Ginny; and what will she do now with him lying stretched a corpse at her feet?'

I surveyed the motley parcel of them, the two others and another who had not yet opened his mouth—a whey visaged fellow—the flunkey and Mr Thomas Cullen all against the door, the mechanics and now others shoving outside, Mother Knapp weeping porter against a little old fellow of considerable belly and a general rusty brown colour wheezing clouds of snuff, and rising like a trumpet above it all the voice of Mrs Britannia approaching with her covey of attendant nymphs. If I was any judge, having some slight knowledge of the dear fair sex, within a minute we should have such a screaming, yellocking and fits of vapours as would curdle your blood and I could not do with it. What I sorely needed was a short time for philosophical reflection, and I cried, 'Be off, all of you,' adding to the flunkey, 'and you, my man, are to stand guard outside.'

'By God,' Mr Dashwood observed, 'this fellow takes a lot on himself.'

Feeling my ever ready choler rising at the rogue's insolence I was about to give him a fine round answer, but the more worthy gentleman interposed, saying, 'No, Jack, come away; we can do no good here.' So it was he himself who got them all out in a plain sensible manner, closing the door and leaving me alone with Maggsy.

As you may expect he was viewing the horrid scene like one of those fearful birds of India which are said to feast upon the dead, and he announced, 'Wait till I tell old Holy Bones about this, I reckon it'll turn him off his lettering for an hour or two. God's Tripes,' he continued, 'ain't he made a bloodsome mess; come to that it's the first I ever see as deaded hisself this way, I wonder why he's got his eyes shut?'

'That circumstance,' I informed him, 'has not escaped my notice,' and the better to attract the little monster's attention I took him by one ear saying, 'take notice, you vampire. You are to go out there and observe. Listen to what you can pick up, if you can make sense of anything they say in all the shrieking and wailing,' which as I had foreseen was now rising to a chorus. 'In special, but private, you are to advise that old bawd of a fruit woman that I desire to have words with her presently and she'll do well for her own good to await my pleasure. And keep your own great trap shut, d'you hear? We've a pretty, teasing mystery on our hands, Master Maggsy.' With that I opened the door, thrust him out into the babel, and was left to my own considerations.

The manner of death is full of curiosities, no two ever being alike; but this one was of peculiar strangeness. The eyes closed, as it were in peace and if you were of a fanciful sort you could almost say a light expression of surprise on the countenance. He had been wearing a powdered tie wig, somewhat old fashioned these days but still affected now and again by the young and elegant, and this lying a little distance away as it had been flung off his head by the explosion and by the pistol ball itself. Seeing the disorder that it was in I turned it about distastefully with the tip of my cane, perceiving that the ball was indeed lodged there, but concluding this must be the surgeon's business.

He had been an elegant young man, if not precisely a buck. A fine neckcloth most curiously folded, the coat no less well cut and of even more genteel material than my own, if that were possible; britches which could only have come from St James's, and boots on which there was not a speck of dust or imperfection in spite of the muck and mire of the streets outside. Nothing out of the way, such as the ridiculous sights you can sometimes now see parading and strutting in the coffee shops these fanciful days, but of a quiet, sober good fashionableness. It was not to my mind the dress of a man who was about to blow the back of his skull out; though to be sure there is no rule as to what you shall wear for that sad occasion. Nor was it the face of one who would choose to take such a drastic leave of the world.

Next I examined the window. The glass fouled with the sulphurous grime of this coal which at times makes London stink like a devil's fart, and there was no mark on it nor any of the panes broken, while the iron bars inside was set fast and hard in the brickwork. There was no good to be had of that, nor did I think there would be; but it is ever my habit in the Art and Science of Detection to consider every smallest thing, and in this manner I returned to the door. There was no better of this for sure enough the key was still on the inside, the lock being shot and the plate or box now torn from the door frame as I had forced it with the weight of my foot. So there you have it. A young man of some elegance—whether of the nobility or gentry I would not be so bold as to say, for bankers are in a class of their own and none knows from whence they come—found shot in a room locked from within and from which there is no other way out.

The appearance must be that he has died of his own hand and there was little doubt that our coroner for this parish, being a resounding barrel who considers himself composed not only of the law but the surgeon's art and the right hand of God Almighty into the bargain, would bring in that verdict plain and simple. For my part I did not

15

believe it. We had here a very fancy fabrication of false evidence, the same pointing to a singular cunning murder, and it were as well to keep my own counsel on it since to speak out too soon would be to warn the villain or villains unknown that I was already sniffing at their heels. Let us play all innocence, I determined, and let 'em think themselves secure to their final destruction. It was a conclusion on which much was to hang; not the least a bold and devilish plot and several as pretty rascals as I ever saw swinging on Newgate Drop.

So resolved I turned finally to examine the instrument of death itself and the claret bottle; the first of these an uncommonly pretty little piece and none of your mere cut throat or highwaymen's weaponry. A gentleman's pocket pistol and for certain one of a pair; a shade over mounted in silver for my liking, as is ever the fanciful Frenchy style, signed by Boutet of Versailles and carrying a ball I judged of only a little less weight than my own more sober English armament. I pondered on this for a space, reflecting on some French interest in the business—for I would put nothing beyond that nation of murderous rascals—before laying it aside for the coroner's officers and taking up the claret bottle.

That was commonplace enough. The indifferent sort they purvey in the Saloon or Mutton Walk here, and with little fresh to tell me. I could see no trace of hair powder on the glass, as some villain might have struck a blow with it, and on tasting a little of the fair third of wine left inside no hint or smell of laudanum or similar mischief. But considering the curious closure of Mr Mytton's eyes I was still not content, and decided on a further test of that claret by a curious and most comic stratagem. Then with nothing more to do here, not sorry to be out of this place, I opened the door just as a fresh altercation arose outside; a honking and gobbling like nothing so much as an old gander in fret.

CHAPTER TWO

An old gander it was, Mr Knyvet the House Manager and much resembling that ill tempered bird in many respects though a shrewd man otherwise. 'What in damnation're you doing here, Boosey?' he was quacking. 'Eh? Your place is front house and well you know it. A carrying naughty messages no doubt, a whore's pander you are,' and then breaking off on seeing me to cry, 'You too, Mr Sturrock. God love us there's mischief afoot if you're about.'

'The mischief's done,' I rejoined. 'A Mr Robert Mytton, as I understand. And looks as if he shot himself.' You will note I always have a nice regard for truth.

'In my theatre?' he demanded. 'The damnation impudence.' With that he thrust open the door as if to give Mr Mytton a piece of his mind, stayed there not above half a minute and came out again as distracted as a gander that's swallowed a stone instead of a frog and can't choke it up fast enough. 'God help us,' he gobbled, 'here's a damnation mess; what's to do about this?'

'Why nothing,' I told him, 'save to send for the coroner's officers, the mortuary men and other interested parties.'

'All the places in London the fool might ha' chose,' he wailed, 'and had to blow his damnation head off in my theatre. They've no thought for others, these young bloods, only their own pleasure. The better part of a guinea to have that place cleaned out, and money's tight, Mr Sturrock; Mr Sheridan'll have the hairs out of my head and my scalp with 'em for this.' I reflected that Mr Sheridan might have weightier matters to think about, but said nothing and our old gander gobbled off on another tack. 'Mr Mytton. Myttons the bankers. Mr Grabble. I see Mr Grabble in the house tonight, very like in the saloon by now,' he announced. 'Grabble can attend to this.'

'And who,' I enquired, 'might Grabble be?'

'Head clerk,' he answered testily. 'To Mr Robert Mytton the elder. Clackerjaw; can't stop talking. Myttons're his business, not mine.' He stopped, stretching his neck like he was set to take a bite out of my nose if he could reach it. 'Mr Sturrock, wasn't you here that time last May, the night His Majesty the King was shot at? You was,' he accused me. 'Always trouble when you're about. I wish to God you'd take your custom somewhere else. Take it to Covent Garden for a change.'

With this he trotted off, leaving me with the man Boosey. A biggish fellow, somewhat straining at his theatre livery and a hardier look about him than these flunkeys commonly have save for his shifty manner; a rogue if ever I saw one. I surveyed him, while from further down the passage there was still a piteous clamour of women and the voice of Britannia instructing them all to have courage and take a drop of gin, and at last said, 'So you're Boosey; a fine old English name it is. Well now, Boosey, it seems your place is the front of the house. So what was you doing here?'

It was on the end of his tongue to give me a dusty answer but seeing my face he changed his mind. 'I was bringing a message; for one of the ladies. That a gentleman'd be waiting in his carriage. For Mrs Britannia,' he volunteered.

'So ho,' I asked, 'she's an accommodating kind, is she?'

'Kind enough, so they say,' he answered. 'And a bouncy ride if you fancy it like that.'

'Come now,' I told him sharply, 'let's not be ungenteel. She's a fine figure of a woman and can afford to be generous. Let's say you was back here on regular business. So did you see anything? I'll tell you the way it is,' I continued with a nice frankness. 'We've no doubt what happened, but there must be a coroner's enquiry and I'm bound to give evidence as the one who discovered the poor young gentleman. I'm particular to have it right.'

'Didn't see nothing. Only that.' He nodded at the dark stain of wine on the floorboards. 'I'm coming for this very room with my message and finds the door locked fast. Thinks there's something amiss and goes on to the gentlemen's general room and calls 'em out. Mr Dashwood and Lilley, and the other gentleman. Then they reckon we should fetch Mr Knyvet and there's three of the stage men here by this time and one of them offers he knows where to find him.'

'Plain and straightforward,' I mused. 'You spoke of a whiff of gunpowder?'

The fellow eyed me sideways. 'So I thought there was at first. It got blowed away in this damnation draught.'

'Very likely,' I agreed. 'Who was the other actor? The one who stood by and said nothing?'

'Mr Digby. Never does say much. Keeps himself apart, and a bit of a dark 'un if you ask me. They say he's got his eye on Miss Virginia Posset, but she don't fancy him.'

'Will that be the young lady old Mother Knapp calls Mistress Ginny?' He nodded, and I observed, 'Well the theatre's ever been the place for love and romance. So you sent for Mr Knyvet. And what then?'

'Why then that horrible boy comes prying round, just as I'm saying about the gunpowder, and he lets out a screech like a demon as there's murder here and he's off to fetch old Sturrock.'

Mentally noting to castigate the little wretch for that impertinence I hauled off on a fresh course. 'You said you didn't see nothing, and the door was locked, as we found. Yet you volunteered it was Mr Robert Mytton in there. How did you know?'

For an instant I thought that shot had struck between wind and water, but the rogue had a ready wit. 'A fair guess. Him being about two or three times a week, waiting on Miss Posset.'

'It seems a young lady in great demand. Was there any others had a fancy for her?'

'It's all musical chairs here. 'Twas common talk she was struck on Mr Dashwood one time but he passed her over to Mr Mytton, having bigger fish to fry.'

'Begod,' I said, 'it's a perfect love nest. Well then, did you hear a shot at any time? Or other disorder?'

'With that damnation roar of cannons and trumpets you wouldn't have heard a thunderbolt. I was out front anyhow.'

'That could be when it happened,' I agreed. 'Now there's this,' displaying the claret bottle. 'How would it come to be in the dressing room? Ain't there rules against that?'

He was indifferent. 'Makes no matter, does it? Might be Mrs Huxey. Or it might be Mr Mytton took it in to pass the time away while waiting.'

There was little more to be said then, for Mr Knyvet came trotting back, now followed by a drunken watchman falling over his staff and lantern with two fellows carrying a scenery door between them. 'What?' he asked, perceiving me again, 'still here, Mr Sturrock? I wish to God you was out of it. And no Mr Grabble neither, seems he's left. Why is't as people you don't want haunt you like blue arsed flies, and them you do are never at hand when you can make 'em useful?'

This was a mischance for I'd have liked a few words and questions with that Mr Grabble, but reflected that there'd be time later on, while Mr Knyvet quacked, 'Have him out quick, men; and you Boosey, go find a sheet or cloth to cover him. Put him in the yard where they can come to fetch him.' Then turning to me he continued, 'Mr Sturrock, please to go away; you're a natural calamity. I'll not have my ladies upset no more; they're in the vapours now and it'll be hysterics next.'

I might have told him that I was the Law and the Law may not be denied, but saw no profit in it as I wanted none of 'em suspicious of me. Upon this indeed there was a fresh uproar down the passage, where more of the actors and a group of Jolly Tars was clustered round that door whence sounds of female grief and Mrs Britannia were issuing. Her own ringing tones, a shriek from Mother Knapp and another from Maggsy; and fast upon it that little monster himself flying out backwards and howling like the devil, Britannia after him in a whirl of muslins with her trident thrust hard up his belly screaming, 'You unnatural, horrid, cruel, wicked little savage.'

'Hold there, ma'am,' I cried, seizing the rogue by the scruff to snatch him away, 'you'll have his hopefuls out. This here's my clerk and servant. Yet if he's offended you I'll see him trounced for it.'

'God's Whiskers,' Maggsy roared, 'she might a took my cobblers out by the roots, a wild ferocious woman she is, I only said his brains was gobbetted all up the wall.'

I landed him a cuff for that which took him sideways and at the same time gained some approval from Mrs Britannia, and though with some care of her indelicate instrument, which was now poking ungenteel at my own most particular parts, I made my bow and announced, 'Your obedient servant, ma'am. And I'd be obliged of a few words with Miss Virginia Posset.'

'Indeed you won't,' she retorted. 'Poor Ginny's in a swooning fit, and I don't wonder. I won't have her troubled no more. I'm surprised at Mr Digby for breaking it so hard, and as for this little monster ...'

Stirred by her generous indignation that naughty trident near enough took away my virtues again, and I stepped back a pace. But I love a ripe, well kindled woman and am always most genteel with such; at least to start with.

I said, 'Then I'll express my sympathy, ma'am, and trouble you no more. It's a vexatious business to be sure.' Miss Virginia Posset could wait too, like Mr Grabble, and I'd very likely get better sense out of her in the end; if I ever thought it worth the trouble. From what I could see now she was stretched upon a sofa with most of the others gathered so close about that they wouldn't do her much good. But I added, 'Then I'll have a gossip with Polly Knapp.'

'God ha' mercy,' this one screeched, 'save me from that thieftaker.'

'Give up,' I told her, 'there's no harm in it, you old fool,' and drew her out into the passage just as Mr Knyvet and his men came past driving all before them, and carrying their sad burden to the accompaniment of more sighs, shrieks, exclamations, etc. Letting them pass, Maggsy then found a little closet stacked with mops, brooms and suchlike, and I pushed the fat bawd into this and said plainly, 'Now, Polly Knapp, you'll answer my questions straight or I might ask which was the last wench you put into service on a screever's letter.'

Now this was but a shot across her bows, to frighten the vile creature that I knew her trade, or one of 'em—namely to put these wenches into places where they could set about a bit of pilfering and sometimes worse—but you'd have thought I'd stuck a knife into her heart. She stared at me agape, her face falling ashen under the raddle, and then bawled, 'God's dear Heart, Mr Sturrock, what're you at? You've set me all in a tremble.'

'Why then,' I said, quick to seize my advantage, 'come take a drink,' and thrust the claret bottle into her mouth and tipped it up, adding 'it'll bring you round.' A pretty philosophical experiment and convenient that the occasion for it had risen so soon.

Coughing and cursing she announced, ' 'Tis claret; it lies windy on the stomach.' Nevertheless she clung to that bottle like a babe to the breast until she had bottomed it, only then pausing to cry, 'You wicked cannibal, that's what was lying against poor Mr Mytton.'

'You'd drink blood if it tasted like liquor,' I observed and demanded, 'why d'you change face so fast when I ask about your wenches?'

The wretch dropped her vapours on the instant and became both cunning and wheedling together. 'Ah, Mr Sturrock dear, you wouldn't set that against me? I look after the pretty dears like a mother.' She crept closer, plucking at my coat buttons, peering fearfully over her shoulder and up at me, weeping porter and whispering, 'Mr Sturrock, dear love, is it certain sure that he done it himself?'

'Done what?' I asked.

'That poor young gentleman. Shot his own head off.'

Perceiving the drift, I might well have asked what made the old bags think it might be otherwise but resolved there would be time for that later too—in this I was mistaken as you shall see—and declared, 'Well, Polly, if you can tell me that some villain could pass through a locked door and then say "Kindly oblige me by opening your mouth, Mr Mytton, while I place the pistol in it," I might have my doubts. But as it is I don't reckon miracles. Mr Robert Mytton shot himself all right; there's no question of that.'

She heaved a great gusty sigh and then rounded on me like a fishwife. 'Then what of God's dear Heart do you want fretting a poor old woman like me?'

'Why, Polly,' I said, all mildness, 'for a bit of gossip, that's all. The facts are certain; what I'm puzzled over is why. And who knows more about Drury Lane than Mother Knapp? So what's this about Miss Virginia Posset and Mr Robert Mytton getting cut off with a guinea, and all the rest of it?'

She fetched up yet another sigh. 'It's like a play on the stage, Mr Sturrock, dear; as good as Mr Sheridan. It's a sad, sweet romance, being as Mr Mytton the elder is well known to piss money and he would have it that the late poor Mr Robert ...' Here dissolving into still more copious torrents and hiccups, it took Maggsy to thump her back and me to bawl at her before we got her on course again and she continued, 'Mr Mytton the elder would have it that his poor dead son should make a match with Lady Dorothea Hookham; which the poor young gentleman don't fancy, as the lady's no pleasure and is well known to have a face somewhat like a horse's arse.'

I held up my hand sternly. 'Pray restrain your observations on the nobility in my presence, Mrs Knapp. I do not approve of 'em. But proceed otherwise.'

'There it is. Old un says to marry the lady or you get cut off with a guinea, but young Mr Robert won't have it. Well then, Miss Ginny was took fancy with Mr Dashwood at one time, but Mr Dashwood thinks if Mr Robert don't want Lady Dorothea why shouldn't he have a try for her himself, then Miss Ginny can make a match of it with Mr Robert and everybody's suited.' The woman let fall another deluge. 'But what could poor Miss Ginny do if Mr Robert lost all his money? Ain't no sense in marrying nothing and she'll never make another Sarah Siddons, poor sweet.'

It made my head spin, but Maggsy remarked, 'So he deaded himself. Like my old master Mr William Makepeace the Practical Chimney Sweeper used to say, you get in between two women and you might as well dead yourself, and he should've known, he got three; but I'd rare like to see that Ladyship if she've got a face like that, I never see a face like that before although ...'

'Silence, you rogue,' I roared, and asked, 'But what's this about a certain Mr Digby?'

The old pander's dugs near enough leapt out of her bodice in agitation. 'Oh, a dark wicked man, that Digby, and mad jealous on account of wanting dear Ginny for himself. You'd not believe what he said to her, dear Mr Sturrock. He said "Well, Ginny, you'll have no good of your latest light of love for he's just gone and blowed his head off."'

'Not the most genteel,' I agreed. 'But how did this tale of Mr Robert Mytton being cut off with a guinea come to get about? He'd be hardly likely to tell it himself.'

'Why from Mr Grabble,' she answered. 'He whispered it to Mrs Huxey; and she whispered it to pretty Ginny as was only right and proper.'

'Well, Polly Knapp, you're a clever woman,' I told her. 'You know the best part about all of 'em. So who was the other gentleman gazing in on that lamentable scene? Oldish and fattish, and not too well placed by the look of him.'

'That old snuff horn?' She sniffed. 'He's no gentleman. That's Dr Blossum; naught but a miserable scribbling writer, a pensioner of Lady Dorothea's. And at daggers drawn with Mr Dashwood, as Mr Dashwood says he's a stinking humbug and the lady should cast him off. Lord,' she cried in a sudden terror, 'it's a damnation lot of questions, Mr Sturrock.'

'Nothing to fret about,' I assured her. 'I'm an uncommon inquisitive man.' I considered her, somewhat vexed that she still showed no sign of falling asleep; it looked as if the claret was innocent enough as, to tell the truth, I had thought it would be. But you should never cast aside a philosophical experiment too early, and I continued in my mildest manner, 'You're overcome, Mrs Knapp, and I don't wonder at it; so my clerk here shall see you to your lodging and carry your oranges.'

Scenting mischief Maggsy grinned at me but Mother Knapp was less willing. 'What?' she demanded, 'that little monster? He'll rape me or cut my throat.'.

'He'll do no such thing,' I told her. 'He ain't big enough, and I'll have the skin off him if he does. Now be off with you, for it's late and there's a thick fog by the look of it.' So I hustled her out, for I could not have put up with another minute of the creature, but Master Maggsy I held back for one last word. 'No tricks,' I said, holding him by the ear. 'You're to be as sweet as one of her whores, d'you understand? But pay attention where she lives and in what company. And above all watch to see whether she falls asleep or drops down dead.'

'Here's a go,' he whispered, all agog, 'have you poisoned the old hunks then?'

'As to that,' I rejoined, 'we shall see; but I fear not.'

Thus ridded of both of them I then composed myself to a moral observation, which I include here gratis; namely, how meretricious is the glitter and tinsel of the front of the theatre falsely hiding the black deeds and blacker schemes behind. Debating then whether to pursue further questions, in especial of that silent Mr Digby, I concluded against for now. I had enough food for thought tonight over a fire and a bottle of Madeira, and it is ever a maxim in the Art and Science of Detection never to start your hares until you know which one to run down and never to cook the prize before he is well and carefully hung. With this profound reflection I set out myself.

There was indeed a noisome fog, and by now all the people had gone either to their sinful pleasures or to inno-cent repose, with never a hackney or torch boy to be seen. After chaffering some minutes with the door keeper for a lantern, which the surly rogue declared he could not find for less than a crown piece, I ended by cursing him roundly and setting forth in the dark and sulphurous stench. My way was simple enough for I had but to pass up Drury Lane and turn across the mouth of Monmouth Street—which might well be called the Entrance to Avernus, for behind this lie the stews of Seven Dials and a fit place for any villainy in such Cimmerian gloom—thus by Old St Giles Churchyard and on to my goal. There is a silence falls on London with these sulphurous humours and a wise man walks carefully, listening behind him;

26

black figures looming out of the murk to be swallowed up again, sometimes a flare of light where the taverns or coffee houses was still plying their trade but most windows shuttered up against the mephitic air, sometimes a carriage with the horses picking their way delicately, and now and again a chair with a torch boy leading the way like a minor demon.

A fit night for any devilment, and I was not to escape unscathed myself. Once or twice I caught a sound of footsteps close behind but stepped on boldly without looking back, for I scorn to act fearful, only settling my beaver and clutching my cane more firmly; this being a treasured relic presented to me by His Majesty the King, God bless him, a Christmas or two back. At St Giles I stopped by a watchman, cowering in a doorway with his lantern and near enough taking to his heels himself when I appeared out of the dark, the poor fool; but the footfalls had stopped then and I continued on my way, the watchman being a fine hero and refusing to light me on. These cowardly rogues are of little use anywhere.

The villains fell on me in the narrowest street, where that pestilential fog was like a blanket. Fortunate for me I heard them again approaching, fortunate also that there were but three of them for I can commonly manage three, or even four at a pinch and have been known to put down five. One of them swinging a cudgel, the which I avoided more by instinct than sight, they came in with a rush; darker shadows in the dark vapour and all wearing masks though you could just discern the lower parts of their faces. I lashed out with my cane at one of these, catching him across the chaps and being rewarded with a curse while I bawled, 'Ho there, watchman!' and brought up my right boot in a wicked pretty stroke at the other's belly which flung him back clasping at himself and screeching and wailing. There is no nicety in London street fighting.

But there was a glint of steel with the third desperado

27

and I perceived that he was wielding a sword stick, a dastardly weapon. This I struck aside the first time, though being worked away from my escape, drove back into a narrow archway where I could be finished off like a badger in a stopped earth. I was as good as lost, yet resolved to sell myself dear as any True Briton should, and I waded in again to the attack getting my rear to the wall and watching that wicked gleam of metal. Once more I struck with my cane, now using it like a spear to keep the rogue at a distance and near enough putting an eye out; but I was hard pressed and that wicked dagger might well have gutted me had not the Hand of Divine Providence been stretched out to my salvation as so often before; yet now in a most peculiar fashion.

Somewhere above a casement was flung open, a voice roared, 'Be damned there, you broiling rogues,' and a sudden stinking flood descended. Being with my back well against the wall I escaped this ambrosial deluge, but the others was most properly drowned and discomfited, cursing and choking and spluttering, and seizing my advantage on the instant I struck one a blow which must have felled an ox, kicked another soundly in the arse and took to my heels. It is a wise part to know when to retreat.

Yet it was an inglorious victory to be saved by a chamber pot and I resolved to say nothing of this mishap, as I am not short of my detractors and jealous enemies who would make it an occasion for rude laughter, especially in the Seven Dials. Nevertheless, secure in my own lodging over a glass of Madeira, I perceived it to be the matter of a most profound moral observation; in short that the Instruments of Providence when He reaches out to succour the righteous are often strange and devious. Thus consoling myself I turned to considering the adventures of the night, and whether this last incident was a matter of simple footpadding, such as is all too common about our streets on dark nights, or whether some one or more of that crowd in the dressing room passage—or others yet unknown—had concluded very correctly that I was not as simple as I professed and set out to have an end of me. You can never tell with these theatrical rascals. They carry their passions off the stage and then magnify 'em into another dramatic play.

It was the better part of a bottle later when Master Maggsy at last appeared. He announced, 'They're horrible low, that lot; if we reckons to be genteel like you keep saying, we'd best run clear of 'em. And I never see such an old tosspot as that Mother Knapp, in and out of one boozer after another all up the Long Acre; she ought've been as pissed as a pudden but give no sign of it, only rolling a bit and wanting to sing hymns with every whore in sight. Partial to whores, she is.'

I rapped sharply with my pipe to bring the contumacious little rascal to order and he continued, 'Likewise if you reckoned to have poisoned the old bladder she had the better of you, for the last I see of her she was stuffing herself with tripes and onions fit to bust and washing 'em down with more porter as merry as a cricket.'

'That was a mere philosophical experiment,' I observed, 'from which we may resolve that the claret itself was innocent enough. What else did you have? And where is the creature's lodging?'

'In one of them courts off Great Earl Street, looked like a whore shop or a night milliners, maybe both, for there was a couple other old crows sitting over the fire and filling some young country wench up with gin, so you know what that means. Didn't have a lot of good out of any of 'em on account of exclaiming and screeching about Mr Robert Mytton, and anyhow that flunkey from the Lane come in soon after.'

'Boosey?' I asked sharpish. 'Does he lodge there too?'

'Seemed more like he was looking for Mother Knapp,' Maggsy replied. 'Fell to going off at her about the booze and said she opened her great parish oven of a mouth too

29

wide and there was them as might shut it for her if she wasn't careful.'

'So ho,' I mused, 'what have we here, I wonder? It's a pretty nest of singing birds. Now consider, Master Maggsy, and remember. Was he wet about the shoulders? Or marked in the face? A cut or bruise?'

Maggsy regarded me suspiciously. 'Have you been afighting again? You're a wild man, Mr Sturrock, you'll get yourself into terrible trouble before you've done; I wisht you'd be more careful. Old Holy Bones swears somebody'll strangle you with your own guts one of these days, and I wouldn't be surprised neither.'

'Master Maggsy,' I reminded him, soft and awful, 'we was talking about the man Boosey.'

'He wasn't wet as I noticed and his face no worse than ordinary; best of times it looks like a murder going somewhere to be done. Anyhow he says what the damnation is I doing there and to take myself out of it or he'll poke his toe up my breech. Which I done.' The cunning little rogue grinned at me. 'Only the window on the court was broke, hung over with a bit of sacking, so I crep up under to hear what was agoing on, and Boosey was riding off at Mother Knapp right and proper and her cussing back at him just as good in between the hymns and the tripes and onions. The upshot of it was he reckons she was agabbing to you a long time, and why was that and did she blab about some wench Nell Ewer, because if she did she's like to get her throat cut.'

'You did pretty fair,' I granted, giving him the bottoms of the Madeira for reward. 'But who is this Nell Ewer?'

'Didn't stop to find out,' he answered. 'Boosey steps over to the door then and stands peering into the court like he's suspectious or waiting for somebody else, and I took myself off into the fog quick. I like a good throat cutting as well as anybody, but not when it might happen to be mine.'

'You're a cowardly little wretch,' I announced, 'and

you might have lost something of import. For mark you, Master Maggsy, how Mother Knapp changed colour when I charged her with putting wenches into service. Yet I cannot conceive that Mr Robert Mytton would entertain any such drab or slut as she could provide.' So musing, and being softened with Madeira, I concluded, 'But let it be; we shall find out. In short, you monster, we have here as pretty a mystery as ever I've seen; and I mean to find the bottom of it.'

CHAPTER THREE

Our Runners, sometimes rudely called Robin Redbreasts, have by custom been under command of the Bow Street Magistracy since the force was first proposed by Mr Henry Fielding in 1749; another of this poor tribe of scribblers and author of the History of Tom Jones and other diverting comedies. In a manner of speaking therefore the Bow Street Magistrate is my master; and being myself a man as believes we should ever show proper deference to them set in authority above us I broached the business to him that next day. Mr Addington however, somewhat testy with the gout, was by no means of the same mind as myself and he observed, 'You take a deal too much pleasure in your own cleverness, Sturrock; the fool shot himself and there's an end of it. Lookee now,' he argued, 'the door locked on the inside. You don't deny that? So do you pretend it was done by some ghost or phantom that escaped by the keyhole?'

'As to that,' I replied, 'the problem lies in the keyhole, but not a ghost escaping through it. Consider, sir,' I urged. 'First, the pistol was lying with Mr Mytton's forefinger still on the trigger. Have you ever tried to put a pistol in your mouth and hold it with your own forefinger placed so?'

'No, by God,' he ejaculated. 'Nor never likely to.'

'It cannot be done. I assure you that the correct and only proper digit for that rash operation is the thumb, the fingers grasping the butt and the pistol held backwards. There's little doubt also that it should have been flung clear by the explosion and convulsion. In short I conclude that the weapon was laid close by the unfortunate young gentleman's hand after the murder was effected.'

Mr A. nodded though somewhat dubiously, and I pressed him, 'Second; the corpse's eyes was closed. Commonly when a man dies so violent the eyes are wide and staring.'

'Must you bring your damnation graveyard talk here?' he demanded. 'Does it mean that much?'

'It might mean a deal. I considered first whether the claret had been drugged or poisoned, but satisfied myself on that score by a simple investigation.' I did not describe my ingenious experiment with Mother Knapp, but continued, 'From this I would say that he was first stunned by a blow on the back of the head; the armament then being placed in his mouth and discharged to finish the job off.'

'God's sake, Sturrock,' Mr A. protested, 'you're turning me up. Go on like this and you'll upset me stomach for the day.'

'Let us not do that, sir. But consider also, Mr Mytton was sitting with mirrors all around so he must have seen who was there. And since there was no sign of struggle my conclusion must be that the villain was some person or persons he expected and had no reason to fear would assault him. And at such time when most part of the theatre was watching that patriotic spectacle, while the uproar of cannons, trumpets, cheers, etc., would cover the shot. As for the claret, that don't signify much and we can dismiss it. Except I fancy it was tipped up as an afterthought, to bring attention that there was something amiss and have the door broke down in the presence of as many witnesses as possible.'

Mr A. shook his head. 'It's too much guesswork.'

'Say rather it's finding the philosophical explanation after casting out all others.'

'Philosophical fiddlesticks,' he said. 'Put that to old

Coroner Fuzz-buzz and he'll laugh like a jackass. You can't get round that locked door.' I kept my own counsel on that, and my master finished, 'He'll bring it in suicide plain and clear.'

'And it'll suit us nicely,' I agreed. 'So our rogues shall think themselves secure. While if we then prove it murder and apprehend the villains concerned it'll take the shine out of our learned coroner's eye. We'll set the whole of London laughing.'

Mr A. gazed at me dumbstruck for a space and at last chuckled. 'You're a damned disrespectful rascal.' Musing on that he chuckled again and added, 'I'd give a dozen of port to see his face if you bring it off. But mind you, I'll not be dragged in. I've had no report or request and it's on your own hands. I'll allow a week's leave of absence and you can go your own way.'

Reflecting that with my Madeira running low a dozen of port would come welcome, I turned next to our clerk, Abel Makepenny. A most excellent old man and also one having a peculiar knowledge of the doings of the nobility and gentry; as I have myself of the wicked ways of the commoner sort. Such a reader of the newsprints there never was before, following all the ins and outs, births, marriages, deaths and bequests like a hound with his nose to a bitch. To him I related the tale while he sat gazing at me like an ancient owl, and at last finished, 'Now then, Abel, this Mr Robert Mytton the elder. How should I approach him?'

He shook his head. 'Bankers is uncommonly difficult to approach at the best of times, and this one more than most. A hard man, so I've heard. His counting house and office in Birchin Lane off Cornhill, and a residence on Brook Street. And there's a whisper as the business is somewhat over extended on account of opening a bank in the West Indies. A mite of head shaking about it in the City. People ain't forgot the South Sea Bubble. I doubt you'll approach Mr Robert Mytton all that easy.'

I said, 'Nonetheless approach him I must,' and asked, 'What of our Lady Dorothea Hookham?'

'Oh dear.' He scratched his nose with his quill in an agitation. 'A fearsome creature, so they say; a woman philosopher and blue stocking.' He lowered his voice. 'They say she's a Bonapartist and a Radical Whig.'

'God's Teeth!' I exclaimed. A Whig I can't put up with at any time, a Radical Whig I abominate, and a female Radical Whig is against all Nature and God's Ordinances.

'Not received at Court,' he announced; which accounted for why I'd never heard of the woman myself. 'And you know how the Prince of Wales expresses himself when displeased. He can't abide the creature.'

'Abel,' I observed, 'we're in deep water here. Yet talk to her I must.'

He shook his head. 'Sooner you than me. But it's simple enough, so I'm told. She holds a kind of soirée or conversazione in the French style each day at five of the clock. A regular ragbag of philosophers, scribblers and other crackpots. All are welcome so long as they talk only of liberty, equality, and suchlike fanciful nonsense. Frenchified notions.' He lowered his voice and asked, 'Jeremy, didn't you say that poor young man was killed by a French pistol?'

'Boutet of Versailles,' I agreed.

Abel nodded, more like an antique owl than ever save that his wig was awry. 'Has it crossed your mind as this might be a matter of Bonapartist spies? And Mr Mytton put down because he got wind of something? It's said on all sides that Portsmouth and London's alive with the rascals.'

To confess the truth I had not considered this. But Abel is an uncommonly sagacious old gentleman, for all he takes a flight of Gothick fancy now and again, and I announced, 'Begod, Abel, you might have hit on something. These Frenchies are cunning rogues and they'd answer for

35

the cleverness of it. I'd best address myself to this lady-ship.'

'She keeps her own establishment on Hanover Square. Her poor old father now never leaves his country seat. He's a bit gone, so I hear.' Abel tapped his forehead. 'Drove so by his own daughter's waywardness most like.'

'There's devilment here,' I said. 'But I'll bottom it.'

With that I next took myself off to find that canting old rogue Holy Moses in Lomber Court. The forenoon not being too far advanced it was now a fine autumn morning, a fair breeze having dissipated the stinking fog of last night, and I walked the length of the Long Acre ben-evolently observing the carriages and curricles with their gay young bloods and high stepping nags, unmannerly dogs of chairmen jostling and bawling, the ladies about their milliners' shops, and street arabs darting amid a lively clatter of hooves and wheels. With the war clouds thickening over Europe there was not a few uniforms about also, fine fellows in the daytime and doubtless heroes on the field of battle, but roaring roisterers at night; as many a lady has often found to her cost what a strange thing it is that a man will so change his manners in the dark.

With that and other profound observations I approached the tenebrous precincts of Seven Dials, that evil purlieu of courts, yards and alleys bounded largely by King Street, Monmouth Street and Castle Street, where the genteel are wise never to venture. Secret tenements huddling close to-gether, shuttered hovels and dens, gin shops, whore shops and worse, and never a sign of an honest man; peopled by all manner of low criminals, ancient crones, drabs, and wicked brats old beyond their years peering at you from dark openings and sometimes pattering after with intent to mischief. It is said that if you have temerity enough you may pass through the length and breadth of the place without ever coming out into daylight, so interconnected with passages, tunnels, and bolts are these foul lodgements;

and it is certain that if once you let your man escape into this warren you have little chance, if any, of ever flushing him out again.

Holy Moses' hovel was of a somewhat better sort than most, for if a screever is to keep the custom of his clients he must set himself up to be a little above the common sort; as having the pox yourself you would not go to a physician also with the pox. Thus you are to see a dark little chamber with the walls not peeling all that much and a handful of sea coal fire in the grate, a worm eaten clerk's writing desk and stool, quills and ink, a few books for the show of it, a sofa with not above most of the guts coming out, and an ancient hour glass by which Moses once measured his sermons and now times his customers. It was here that out of my open handed benevolence I was laying out six pennies a week on Master Maggsy's education.

Both he and Holy Moses was hard at their letters as I arrived, and the old rogue fell into affectation of transports at seeing me. Still with an air of canonical rosiness about him, though most of it was gin, he rolled up his eyes to the whites and cried, 'Here's a condescension to visit us, Mr Sturrock; it makes light of our day and blesses our labours. As I never cease to tell this child of sin, what a benefactor you are to keep his feet upon the paths of righteousness when but one step aside leads to the eternal fire. *"Facilis descensus Averno"*; how easy is the descent to Hell. Virgil.'

'Quite so,' I said, 'but we've no time for learned disquisitions. I've work for you.'

'For how much?' he asked, looking above ordinary cunning.

'To keep yourself on the right side of me,' I told him. 'Cast your mind to one, Mother Knapp; a fruit seller at the Drury.'

He rolled his eyes Heavenwards again and wept. 'Oh that ravisher of innocence; that snare for chastity. And now this sad and lamentable and most sinful act at the

37

Drury last night.' The old hypocrite's eyes descended again, peering and somewhat fearful behind the tears. 'What have we here, Mr Sturrock?'

I studied him narrowly but said, 'Why nothing. That was suicide and no concern of mine. But Polly Knapp's about some business and I want to know what it is. Likewise what she's up to with a wench called Nell Ewer.'

'Nell Ewer?'

He blenched to the lips as if the Angel of the Lord had dropped in of a sudden to tell him that the fire was lit and the toasting spit ready. As guilty as I ever saw a man, and being in no mood for niceties I took him by the neck cloth for an admonitory throttle. 'Nell Ewer,' I repeated. 'Come now, you weeping rogue, what d'you know of the slut?'

'As God's my judge,' he screeched, half strangled. 'Oh dear me, Mr Sturrock. *"Mens sibi conscia recti"*, I have a mind conscious of its rectitude; yet have I been in error, I wonder?'

'Moses,' I told him, 'you live in error; and we can easy set it right. What about this wench?'

'A letter, Mr Sturrock,' he wept 'No more. Three weeks back I wrote a letter for her at Mrs Knapp's instruction.'

'So ho,' I said. 'And what was it?'

'To commend her as honest, virtuous, obedient and industrious, and put forward by a lady of quality in Wiltshire, now forced to turn Nell Ewer away on account of leaving for India with her husband and wishful to find the girl another place in service.'

'Moses,' I observed, 'we know your trade and I could see you in Newgate for it. But you've written many another letter like that. What's so strange about this one?'

'This fearful death at the Drury,' he quavered. 'And where that letter was intended for. It was superscribed "To whom it may concern", but Polly Knapp, then being a little drunk and merry, let out that it was for a Mrs Elspeth,

38

housekeeper to Mr Robert Mytton the elder, in Brook Street. Alas, Mr Sturrock, what have we here?'

As to that I wondered myself, and was to wonder more, but then said plainly, 'Why nothing. What could some drab or slut have to do with Mr Mytton? Nonetheless I want to know what she and Mother Knapp are up to. And you shall find out for me.'

'Me?' he demanded, as tearful indignant as a maiden snatching at her drawers. 'How can I, Mr Sturrock? I can't and daren't.'

'You can and must,' I retorted. 'Moreover you'll set about it now, and you'll report to me this night at the Brown Bear Tavern.'

'He'll get his tripes cut out for it,' Maggsy announced with some relish.

'Be silent,' I told the little monster and, leaving Holy Moses to his lamentations, drew him away about the next part of the day's business; the first being Mr Hackett's Eating House by the brewery off Broad Street, where I took a light repast of a pound or so of sirloin, an apple pie with Stilton and a quart of porter while Maggsy as you might expect gobbled everything within sight. Then I gave him his instructions as to certain enquiries he was to make at Drury Lane, and after that in the stable mews at Brook Street, and packed him off about them. For myself I rested for a while, studied the latest intelligences in *The Times* and *The True Briton*, reflected on this dark mystery—which I will confess I had little light on as yet—and at length repaired at an easy walking pace to Hanover Square.

A most elegant commodious quarter with handsome residences and a nicety of pillars and porticos lately built in the modern style, as the nobility and gentry are now moving out of the middle parts of London to the sweeter airs of the west. There was a carriage or two and a phaeton drawn up outside one establishment and a knot of chairmen lounging against the railings as these rude fellows so often do, like post boys and hackney drivers having little or no respect for their betters. But I am not to be discommoded by the lower sort and I ascended the steps to execute a discreet flourish on the knocker; and when the door was opened by a handsome fellow in dark livery and powdered wig announced, 'To wait upon Lady Dorothea Hookham. Dr Jeremy Sturrock, of philosophy; late from Boston, the Americas.'

He bowed respectfully and led me across a pretty, pillared hall with a domed ceiling and tiled floor, marble stairs with a gilt finger rail and several most elevated pictures after the Italian style. Here at a half opened door it appeared some ceremony must be observed for there was a woman holding forth within, and the servant stayed me until she should have finished speaking. Thus arrested I had leisure to survey the scene; an equally elegant salon decorated and furnished after the manner of Mr Adam, with fine tall windows, fanciful plaster work, modish light colouring and ivory woodwork, and everywhere speaking of wealth and refined taste; a change indeed from the squalors of Seven Dials.

There was a dozen or so people present, sitting with dishes of tea but all turned to the woman, or indeed Hypatia, who was plainly queen of the occasion. Of a biggish stature and dressed to the mode, yet of a sober manner, and undoubtedly somewhat resembling a horse but by no means of the hinder parts as that lewd and fanciful Mother Knapp had pretended; a pale complexion and mouse coloured hair, but uncommonly fine dark and speaking eyes which redeemed her plainness. Yet not a woman for the bedchamber, I concluded.

Save for one other, an elderly lady much resembling a little grey parrot and seemingly of small interest in the proceedings being engaged about some needlework, all the others was men; most of a genteel or even foppish appearance, but also that old, fat and snuff coloured Dr Blossum who had been present at the Drury last night, Mr Jack Dashwood, his companion Nicholas Lilley, and Mr Tom Cullen. Food for thought once more and plainly my disguise or subterfuge was soon to go up in a puff of gunpowder smoke, but I stood my ground watching them while the woman continued her peroration; this seemingly in praise of that fanciful French rogue, Jean Jacques Rousseau and such a taradiddle of nonsense as made my ears burn. But at last she was done and looked across to me and the servant, who then announced, 'The Dr Jeremy Sturrock, my lady. Philosopher. Late of the Americas.'

She turned on me a kind, and I must confess, singularly sweet smile, saying, 'Then come and join us, Dr Sturrock, and welcome.' At this Mr Dashwood twisted in his chair to gaze, while Lilley looked open mouthed, even Mr Tom Cullen appeared amazed, and the old snuff coloured pot belly made a kind of turkey gobbling noise. But all unconscious of this the lady said, 'We were disputing, sir, on the nature of equality, the natural sinlessness of man in a virtuous society, and the aim of every revolution to achieve that happy state.'

Now I will own that I spoke somewhat out of turn, but I cannot and never could abide this kind of addlepated prattle, moreover since the explosion was bound to come any minute it were just as well to lay the train myself, and I announced, 'If it comes to equality, ma'am, I know not what it is for I never saw any yet; maybe some day one of your philosophers may show me a bit in a pickle jar. For sinlessness I never saw that either since man is born to sin as he is to death. While as to revolution it is a business which once begun you cannot stop, commonly started by a few crackpots and more knaves, and mostly to the great suffering of innocent people who want no part of it.'

One of Maggsy's own gems could not have produced a more profound silence; until the old doctor let out a sound midway between a belly laugh and a great belch of snuff,

41

and Mr Dashwood announced, 'You're imposed upon, Dorothea; this lout's an impostor. Allow me to present the fellow. A common thieftaker, a hangman's tout; one Jeremy Sturrock of Bow Street. We had the pleasure of viewing him about his business at Drury Lane last night.' He made a most ineffable theatrical gesture with his kerchief, like blowing the stink away, and added, 'Sounding and resembling little so much as an empty porter jug in a greatcoat.'

For an instant I felt the oncome of a seizure, while that booby Mr Lilley gave a horse snicker and the wiser Mr Cullen expostulated, 'Now, Jack.' Perhaps what followed was somewhat less than nice gentility in presence of the nobility, but my choler had the better of me and I retorted, 'Porter jug yourself, sir; indeed as I observed your own performance I would say that when you raised your right hand had you but placed the other on your hip you had most perfectly resembled a coffee pot.'

There was a hush once more, broke only by Dr Blossum giving another great guffaw but choking on it, then Mr Dashwood casting his chair back and taking a stiff kneed step towards me. For my part I dared the impudent jackanapes, and God knows what the end might have been had not my lady cried out imperiously, 'Gentlemen!'

Dashwood bowed to her as stiff as a ramrod, saying, 'Your pardon, ma'am. Yet I require you to call your man and have this bumpkin put out.'

This plainly nettled the lady, being a commanding female, and she enquired, 'You require me, Mr Dashwood?'

'Why yes, ma'am,' he replied, 'I do. Else I shall leave myself.'

'Why then,' she replied, more commanding than ever, 'so you shall. And I shall observe that you yourself offered the first insult. We shall welcome you again gladly when your temper's a little cooled, Mr Dashwood.'

Even then the poor fool must needs make it worse for

himself. He cried, 'God's Teeth, Dorothea, the man's an impostor I say. The sweepings of Bow Street.'

'So he shall explain himself to me,' my lady said, and then finished royally: 'You may all leave us, gentlemen.'

Once more he bowed; without another word turned to march out followed by his fellow Lilley and Mr Cullen, who stopped by me with an uncommon hard look on his face—which I was sorry for as I had somewhat taken to him—and said, 'That was ill spoken, Mr Sturrock. Nobody could blame poor Jack wanting satisfaction for that.'

'If you please, Mr Cullen,' my lady reproved him. 'I do not choose to have my drawing room turned into a bear garden or tavern.'

There was no denying the woman, and leaving me standing like a naughty schoolboy, not daring to look at me for fear of the schoolmarm's cane, they all rose obediently. All save Dr Blossum who muttered as he passed me, 'Good, sir; choice. Choicely good. I'll have all London laughing over that tonight,' then cast one backward glance at the mistress and scuttled out with the others.

So left alone with her and the little old parrot lady for duenna I said, 'I ask your pardon, ma'am, most humbly. And I'll own it was not my best style of wit.'

The older woman lifted one bright eye at me from her needlework, though whether amused or in reproof I could not tell, and Lady Dorothea continued, 'It was not well done. And may I ask the meaning of this subterfuge? Dr Sturrock, indeed.'

I could scarcely tell the woman it was so as to observe without warning the company she kept, and told her, 'To be plain with you I feared that had I approached as mere Jeremy Sturrock of the Bow Street Runners I might not have been admitted. The Runners are not commonly welcomed in genteel establishments, and I thought it best not to state my business before servants or in public.'

She frowned at me, but asked, 'And what is that?'

'Ma'am,' I said, 'I would not wish to speak one word which might cause you grief or discomfort. It is touching the death of Mr Robert Mytton.'

For an instant a veil lay over those fine eyes before she murmured, 'Poor Robert,' and then continued, 'I'm not likely to fall into the vapours, Mr Sturrock.'

Begod I did not think the creature could even if she tried, nevertheless I still chose my words to a nicety. 'The common report is that Mr Mytton died by his own hand. That is not true, ma'am.'

The ancient duenna peered over at me seemingly not all that surprised, while Lady Dorothea tightened her lips a little, and I recounted the whole tale omitting only those matters which might distress even such an iron souled female as this, answering all their questions and exclamations so far as I thought fit—which was not all that far and no names mentioned—and at last concluding, 'So there's nothing else for it, ma'am. He was made away with for reasons presently unknown, by some villain or villains also unknown, and if we're to see these same villains brought to justice there are certain things I must ask.'

'No, but damme, Dorothea,' the old lady cried. 'This man's somewhat more than over bold.'

'Let be, Harriet,' Lady Dorothea told her. Gazing into the fire she did not speak again for a while but then sighed and continued, 'Neither could we think Mr Mytton would do such a thing. He wasn't a man of that mind. But what do you want of me, Mr Sturrock?' She looked at me very straight. 'You wish to know my own relation with Mr Robert Mytton?'

I bowed, even as Miss Harriet again cried, 'Now, damnation, Dorothea; this goes beyond all bounds. D'you want your business the talk of Bow Street?'

'I see no harm in it,' that astonishing woman replied. 'It has been of the drawing rooms for months. To be plain, Mr Sturrock, our respective fathers would have it that we

44

should marry. Robert, however, was of another mind.' For an instant there was a look in her eyes of the grief that she was too proud or too crackpot philosophical to admit.

'Fiddlesticks,' Miss Harriet snapped. 'If you're bent on speaking blunt, Dorothea, be damned so shall I. He'd ha' taken you, and well you know it, had you but climbed down off your high horse.'

'I would not have had him sleeping on a coalfield,' Lady Dorothea answered.

Never had I met a brace of females like this before, but since they were talking so free they might as well go on with it and I asked, 'A coalfield, ma'am?'

Just as openly she told me, 'There is a survey of coal and iron on certain of my father's estates in the Midland Counties. I do not approve of such things; they are ruination for our people who look to us for their care and their land, but Mr Robert Mytton the elder wants that coal and iron, while my own poor father wants a husband for his only daughter.' She favoured me with a smile, again tinged with sadness. 'Who is already growing elderly for the market; and a market it is, Mr Sturrock.'

'Fiddlesticks,' Miss Harriet announced once more, and for good measure added, 'Candle knobs.'

Dumbfounded by her plainness, wondering even whether the poor creature was not a little comical in the head from prolonged spinsterhood and Whiggish notions, I said, 'You honour me by so much confidence. But to be more general do you know of any who might have had an enmity to Mr Mytton? Or why they should have?'

'I do not,' she answered. 'If I did I would tell you.'

For my own part I could think of one for certain if only a half of the Drury Lane gossip and this tale of coalfields were true, but I observed, 'Then I must look elsewhere,' and asked flatly, 'ma'am, will you do me a service? It would be well for me to have words with Mr Robert Mytton the elder, but from what I hear of that gentleman he's not easy to come at. Will you write me an introduction, stating the case and commending me to him?'

'If you think it any matter. Though I will warn you that Mr Mytton very likely has no further interest in me now.' Nevertheless she crossed over to her writing desk between the tall windows and busied herself for a few minutes scratching with a quill while I sat silent, aware that Miss Harriet was eyeing me keenly over her needlework. But she said nothing and at length Lady Dorothea came back bearing the paper, asking, 'Will that do?'

She had writ, 'Sir; I commend the bearer, Mr Jeremy Sturrock, to your attention. Mr Sturrock has conveyed certain matters to my attention concerning the death of your son (and my own very dear friend) which I consider ought to be brought to light, both as regards your own comfort of mind and Robert's memory. That memory is now also my own concern, and as one who might have stood in closer relationship but is now robbed of it by this cruel blow I request you to hear Mr Sturrock out. With respect, Dorothea Hookham.' And very genteel, I considered; crackpot she might be, but also an uncommon clever woman who knew how to lay on the butter where it would do the most good.

So having done as well as I expected I rose to take my leave but said finally, 'There is one last matter. With respect I shall advise you to keep our business today the strictest secret. The coroner will find that Mr Robert Mytton died by his own hand; so we must let it rest for now. And if it can be put about that I came here to enquire most impudently into his private affairs, as why he should take his own life, but got sent off with a flea in my ear, so much the better.'

Lady Dorothea frowned at me. 'Do I understand that you suspect some person in this house today? My friends?'

That was the last bee I wanted her to get in her bonnet; for this present the less said or asked about any of her fine

46

Whiggish company the better. 'I'd never think of such a dreadful thing,' I hastened to assure her. 'But if that tale gets back to Drury Lane it'll do no harm.'

Plainly not liking the deception she frowned still more, and Miss Harriet demanded, 'And so have Mr Mytton branded as a suicide? What of his immortal soul?'

'I'm persuaded his soul would sooner have its revenge. And no doubt the Lord will see the matter in its true light, ma'am,' I said. 'As He'll lead us to the light also, with my help and so long as we don't warn the villains that I'm after 'em.'

With that moral and salutary remark I left them, not ill contented. Little enough achieved, but something; and, as my old sea captain friend will often say, better bail one pannikin of water at a time than toss the boat keel over tip trying to throw it all out at once.

CHAPTER FOUR

When I returned to my lodging it was to find Master Maggsy there before me, lording it in my own chair, smoking one of my pipes, my best tobacco into the bargain, and sampling my Madeira; this last being the gift of a dozen bottles from a most excellent gentleman, now my very good friend but not always so, Sir Tobias Westleigh. The pipe I wrapped around Maggsy's ears, breaking it, and the Madeira I drank off myself while reading the little villain an improving lecture on thievery, the cost of good Broseley pipes, the abusement of a kind master, intemperance and doubtless he'd turn to wenching next if he wasn't already, etc. That being accomplished I asked him, 'Now then, what good did you have of your work?'

'Done very well, doing it all for you I am,' he announced sulkily. 'Got my head smacked by one of the mechanics at Drury Lane, and got into a fight with one of the boys who rolls about under the sea to make Britannia's waves, he reckoned that was worse'n chimney sweeping and I said it weren't because you didn't get your arse singed when servants forgot to let the fire out soon enough and left the chimney hot. But he couldn't tell me much, so after that I loosed off a big bag of sand hanging on a rope at one of the other mechanics when he wasn't looking, and then screeched at him to stand clear which he did and very near cried over me saying I'd saved his skull; which I had, and he give me a drink of porter. I like this life I do; I hope you don't get yourself murdered too soon.'

'There's a fair danger you'll get murdered first,' I

48

observed through my teeth. 'Come to it, you rogue.'

'I'm atelling you. They all reckon the deader deaded himself all right, though this mechanic says he couldn't've been there to meet Miss Posset as she'd turned him over because he'd lost all his money. This mechanic's name is Maggs, near enough the same as mine and I hope to God he ain't my dad and I don't know, because I don't fancy the look of him; he's a mean little runt and got a down on everybody, particular Mrs Britannia on account she keeps reckoning her throne squeaks when she sits on it, and he claims it squeaks because she's got an itchy backside and can't sit still on account of being a very rollicksome woman; he says she'll rollick with anybody who fancies a ride.'

'Master Maggsy . . .' I said in an awful voice.

'You're a most awful impatient man,' he complained. 'If somebody don't have your tripes out one of these days you'll be took of a seizure first. That Maggs was the best I could've picked on account he knows everything about everybody. Well then, there was another of the stage men come in this morning with a kind of ragged cut down his face; wouldn't say how he got it but Maggs reckoned some doxy must've tried to claw his eye out.'

'So ho,' I said. 'His name?'

'Jake Tasker. Wicked bastard so Maggs said, but didn't get a sight of him myself on account he wasn't there then.'

'Nevertheless we must make occasion to see Mr Tasker,' I mused. 'What else?'

'The flunkey Boosey's gone and upped and left the Drury; told Mr Knyvet the manager he was on a better lay, and Mr Knyvet could stuff his livery the best place he fancied it. Ain't much about Mr Digby the actor, save he was aiming to work himself between Miss Posset's legs but she wouldn't have him, and he can commonly be found in Ned's Coffee House off the Lane. As for Mr Tom Cullen, Maggs don't know nothing about him, which is a miracle, except somebody told Maggs he was something to do

49

with people named Isaacs and Fettelson. Dunno who they might be; no more does Maggs.'

'Isaacs and Fettelson is another firm of bankers,' I said very soft. 'What the devil have we here, I wonder? And the old Dr Blossum?' I asked.

'Maggs don't go much on him, seems he's an old scrivener who gets let into the theatre for nothing so long as he writes a good piece about the play; but Maggs says the woman as serves pies and suchlike in the Mutton Walk might know more, she sometimes giving him bits to eat when they shut up at night. So I tell her as I've found a snuff box and I wondered if he might give me a shilling if I took it back to him; and she says the poor old soul'd be more like to hope somebody'd give him a shilling instead, but for what it was worth he lodges in Grub Street, the Fore Street end out of Cheapside.'

'So now we have a Grub Street scribbler in the business,' I mused. 'You did pretty well, Master Maggsy; not the worth of a new clay pipe and my Madeira, but well enough. What did you find in Brook Street?'

'Done well there too,' he announced. 'Looks like they've had one murder already, not counting the deader last night. Servant wench. Got runned over with a carriage and kicked by the hosses.'

He continued, 'I come upon a stable lad in Three Kings' Yard round back of Brook Street where all the gentry has their stables and coaches. He was sitting on a muck heap and near enough weeping with the toothache; face like a pig's bladder he'd got and I offered to knock his tooth out for him, but he didn't fancy that. Seemed he was a bit simple so I let on I'd got a sister who was something wonderful with toothache; I told him her cure for it and he near enough pissed himself with laughing, and then I said it so happened she was looking for a new situation and she was always particular obliging with anybody as did her a kindness, and specially partial to a rollick with a fine

50

stable boy. So did he think it was any good her trying at Mr Mytton's, which I'd heard was a most genteel establishment. Well, he knowed Mr Mytton's all right.'

I shall not weary you further with Maggsy's lewdness, but the substance of his tale was that, according to this boy, the kitchen wench from Mr Mytton's had set out on her lawful or otherwise occasions one night about a month since, and had then fallen or been pushed beneath a carriage and horses. Whereupon, being taken to the Pauper Hospital, she had died of a broken head; and Mr Mytton himself had subscribed a shilling towards her funeral complaining of the expense and the wench's thoughtlessness. Two or three days after this sad event another woman had appeared, presented a letter of recommendation, and been taken on; this one, as you will not be surprised, being Nell Ewer and by the stable boy's account a pretty piece, all dimples and demurity, but very likely a naughty trollop if the truth was known.

This I considered more than likely myself, though whether it had any part of Mr. Robert Mytton's death were another matter. But the tale thus being recounted, with several observations of my own and certain food for thought, we settled to a hearty supper of one of Bellamy's excellent veal pies and finally set out about our next occasions; these being the Brown Bear Tavern and our canonical rogue, Holy Moses. A black stinking night again, and Master Maggsy attending with a lantern as much to keep him apart from my Madeira as to light me through the fog; myself armed with a heavy blackthorn cudgel rather than His Majesty's light and elegant cane.

For your better understanding the Brown Bear is what is known by the vulgar as a flash house, or a house where stolen goods are sold and received, information exchanged, and all manner of devilments concocted; in short the haunt of a pretty company of villains and their drabs, the most part all the better of a good hanging. Not by no means a rendezvous for the genteel and a precise lady would fall into vapours at the spectacle, but useful to me as many of these little lambs will often bleat fast enough if they fancy they feel the hemp tickling their necks.

Arriving there safely we ensconced ourselves prudently with our backs against the wall, placing my cudgel on the board where it could be seen, and calling for a pot of mulled claret for myself and the same of small beer for Maggsy. A scene such as might have stayed even Mr Hogarth's pen. The bold eyed serving wench with her tits pretty well as open to all as her looks, a reek of fog and tobacco smoke, an assemblage of rogues sitting as dark as their own misdeeds in the candlelight, some of them staying their thieves' kitchen talk to gaze sidelong at me; walls that hadn't seen a lick of whitewash in a dozen years and timber very near as black as the Devil's fundament. Moreover Holy Moses was not yet present and I do not like to be kept waiting by a rogue.

He crept in at last, however, sidling through the press in his rusty black greatcoat, muffler tied up to his eyes and moulting old beaver. 'What a den is this,' he moaned, casting up his eyes, 'what a sink of iniquity. I grieve that a man of your excellence should condescend to it.'

'So long as you never grieve for nothing worse you'll come to no harm,' I announced, hammering for the wench with my cudgel and calling for a quart of spiced ale. 'What good did you have of Mother Knapp?'

'And what a shameless, overflowing wench,' he observed, giving a dolorous sigh but viewing her mischievously nonetheless. 'What good would any righteous man have of that vessel of sin? I perceive, Mr Sturrock, that you yourself are imbibing mulled claret.'

'Why so I am.' I affected some surprise at the circumstance but said, 'Spiced ale and be glad of it. Come now; what of Mrs Knapp? And Nell Ewer?'

Up went his eyes to Heaven again. 'You are a hard man,'

he complained. ' "*Si fractus illabatur orbis impavidum ferient ruinae*", if the skies were to break and fall, the ruins would strike him undismayed. Horace.'

'Be damned to your Latinizing,' I rejoined, 'come to Nell Ewer.'

He looked at me sideways, taking a dive into his ale and damned near bottoming it before coming up for wind. But the old rascal had something in his noddle for certain. He cried, 'Mr Sturrock, I am perturbed. A pot of mulled claret would comfort me.'

'That be damned,' I observed. 'You're more like to get yourself a transport to Botany Bay. Out with it, Master Moses, or I'll see you in leg irons myself.'

'What a vile place is London,' Moses wept. 'Mrs Knapp was somewhat in her cups. And when I enquired of her was she putting some poor simple country child to London service she laughed near enough to choke herself.' He sighed dolorously again, gazing into his empty pot and then sideways at me once more. 'She let fall a name in her unseemly merriment. In short, Mr Sturrock, she said if you could call Antimony Nell a poor simple country wench the Devil himself would turn a saint.'

'What's this?' I enquired. 'Is that how the trollop's known?'

He nodded dolefully. 'It would appear so.'

'Antimony,' I mused. 'Tartar emetic. Causing collywobbles of the belly and even death if taken enough. Commonly used to condition horses, but sometimes also by unkind ladies who wish to allay their husbands' lechery when it might be untimely. And sometimes by whores when they aim to take their customer's pay but not render the service. What of damnation have we here, I wonder? One servant wench killed and this other put in to take her place. Come, Master Moses,' I demanded, seizing him by the neck cloth the better to make it plain, 'What more do you know?'

'Nothing,' he protested. 'I swear it. I was told plain to ask no questions and keep my throat safe. As God's my judge I know nothing of what these wicked people are about.'

'Take care He don't judge you untimely,' I warned the rascal. 'We've a pretty business here by the look of it, though not even I can see what it means as yet.' But I hammered on the board again for the wench to command another pot of claret and one more quart of ale in my kindness, and then demanded, 'What did you hear of the man Boosey?'

He took the ale sadly, still muttering some improper nonsense about claret but at last confessing, 'As to Boosey, I am engaged to pen two letters for him. One from the widow of a naval captain commending him as a brave and loyal servant, the other from a gentleman as he saved from footpads on Hounslow Heath, so recovering and handing back to the same gentleman a purse containing twenty guineas.'

'What of God's Name is afoot?' I asked. 'Is this some part of the business with Nell Ewer?'

'I do not know,' he avowed. 'I know nothing save that I meet Boosey at the Long Acre Tavern tomorrow afternoon.'

'And so you shall,' I said. 'You shall write those letters, Master Moses, and you shall find out where he means to take 'em.'

'I cannot, Mr Sturrock,' he protested, 'I dare not. You'll be the death of me.'

But before I could instruct him what truly would be his death, Maggsy cried out, 'God's Whiskers, here's a bit of fun,' and a more singular uproar arose. It was a rude spectacle; a parcel of low rogues having got the serving wench across a table and sporting with her, she with her bodice half pulled off and her clouts up about her waist, waving her legs and yellocking and laughing while the

horrible villains howled coarse jests, Sailor Tom the land-
lord bawled, 'Belay there, you dogs,' laying about him with
a candle holder, and Master Maggsy jigged up and down
on the bench screeching. 'They'll have her stripped bare in
a minute.' For my part I ignored this ungenteel scene, dragging Holy Moses closer by his muffler and roaring in his
ear above the clamour, 'Now you prating, preaching, canting Latinizer, you'll do as you're told.'

I gave him a hearty shake for good measure and he
whimpered, 'Let me be, Mr Sturrock, I want no part of it,'
while at that same instant Maggsy screeched louder still
and dragged me sideways with a jolt. That instant also
something flew shining between Moses and me and hung
quivering in the woodwork, as for one more instant we sat
gazing at it with the din continuing unabated, the wench
screaming 'Rape!' and Maggsy whispering, 'Sweet Jesus,
that near enough filleted you.' It was a heavy bladed
throwing knife buried three inches deep in the wood, and
had it struck either of us would have split his head or mine
like an apple. Moses gave vent to a sound like an expiring
pig and slipped off the bench and under the table, but I am
made of sterner stuff; and was moreover enraged.

Seizing my cudgel and thrusting out I advanced into the
fray, while Maggsy clung to my coat tails beseeching,
'Come back, you damned old fool, they'll gut you.' But I
was of no mood for advice, nor can my pen describe the
bacchanalian scene which by now was become a general
battle. That shameless wench lying with her tits naked
and belly exposed, shrieking and choking and laughing,
two or three of the rogues trying to pour a pot of ale down
her throat, others of them clinging to her arms and legs
bawling indecent instructions and yet more fighting to get
at 'em; likewise Sailor Tom staggering with a bloody nose
but coming back to wield a bottle, the clatter of watchmen's rattles outside though not daring any closer, as they
never do, the cowardly rats. Scenting new mischief one

black bearded rogue took a swing at me with a pot but him I laid cold with a blow from my cudgel, performed the like pacific service for another, and seized one more by his filthy neck-cloth in my left hand as like throttling him as breaking his neck, while Sailor Tom roared, 'Lay off, you scum, you'll have the place afire.'

Not to relate too much of this vulgar occasion, I laid another one or two of 'em low though hardly sure why I was engaging myself at all, for there was little hope of finding the villain who had flung that knife, and I had no great thought of saving the wench; let her take all she was asking for and plenty of it. Moreover Maggsy himself peered from under a table where he was sheltering from the storm and cried afresh, 'Come out of it I say, there's two or three of 'em here and you'll get another knife in your guts in a minute, I see the one as chucked the first and he's got clear away.' Moreover Sailor Tom paused for a moment after splitting another with a bang from his bottle, apostrophized the wench, 'If you want 'em, you poxy strumpet, have 'em outside,' and added to me, 'God's sake get out of this, Mr Sturrock, it ain't no business of yours; the lads is playful tonight, they'll fillet you.'

So I suffered myself to withdraw from the fray, meeting Holy Moses creeping on all fours along the wainscot and weeping in terror. Thus we emerged to the street with that noisome fog swirling about us, yellow in the light of windows and doorway, with the useless watchmen peering in fearfully at the broilsome spectacle. Them I tried to encourage, speaking roundly of public order and their duty, etc., but they answered, 'Go piss yourself, master, you'll need a troop of militia to order this lot,' and Maggsy chattered, 'I don't like it neither, can't see a dog's arse from his nose, and that knife throwing bastard could be awaiting for us anywhere, keep away from the light of the door, Mr Sturrock, for God's sake, and let's make off.'

'Am I surrounded by cowards?' I demanded.

'By the Grace of God you are,' Holy Moses exclaimed, 'and I'm one of 'em; I stay not here.' He sighed a gust of spiced ale in my face. 'One of us is marked for certain, me or you.' And with that he vanished as if the fog had swallowed him alive.

'Let's get out of it ourselves,' Maggsy urged, 'I don't like knives, never did; it's a nasty feeling when they grates into your guts.' Being a little out of patience I was half inclined to return to the engagement, which was now the appearance of a very fair riot with the wench herself now laying about her and near as naked as Diana, but perceiving that there was small profit and less sense to be got out of that unruly crew I consented to retreat. 'And about time too,' Master Maggsy grumbled. 'Ain't you never satisfied? God's Truth, you laid two cold, throttled one more and near enough crippled another for life, that ought to be enough even for you; I wish you'd get it into your head that you don't go about to make people like you.'

'The esteem of rogues and villains is but the crackling of thorns under a pot,' I observed as we passed into the murk, leaving that ungenteel uproar behind. 'Come now, what did you observe?'

'I see the whole thing. The little'n as slung the knife was away like a skinned eel as soon as he loosed it off. Darkish face and an eye patch, shiny black straw hat like some of the sailors, and sea boots. Took the knife out of the leg of his boot. God's Tripes, I never see anything so quick in my life.'

We passed into Covent Garden, where there was a few torches burning in the surrounding obfuscation, and he continued, 'Three of 'em come in after old Holy Bones and stopped over by the beer barrels; it was a put up job all right. The two big 'uns worked over to where that wench was serving, and one tipped a pot of beer down between her tits, and when she come round to hit a swipe at him the other tossed her on the table back down and pulled her

57

clouts up, and the first started the mill. Then everybody joined in and I reckoned it was a nice bit of fun save I catched sight of the little 'un again and he was still against the beer barrels till they was all at the rollicking and not taking any notice, and then up come the knife. Thought you was a deader, I did; I thought God A'mighty, there goes my bread and butter.'

'A most selfish and improper consideration,' I said. 'Who was it intended for, me or Moses? Much might hang on that.'

'Couldn't tell,' he answered indifferently. 'I just see it coming; but there's one thing sure, if I hadn't pulled you aside you'd have got spitted like a magpie. I wisht we was well out of this lot, if you ask me I reckon you've bit off more'n you can chew, and it ain't no Bellamy's veal pie neither.'

'The day I ask you,' I admonished him sharply, 'and the day Jeremy Sturrock bites off more than he can chew, you may go and sing choir in St Paul's Cathedral, that being an equally unlikely event.'

With few people about and what carriages there was going sober, most having a torch boy to lead them, we took our way discreetly while listening for footfalls behind us in this dark and pestilential fog; I fear no man living in front of me yet mislike a rogue coming from the back. But we reached my chambers safely and there, when Master Maggsy had lit the candles, I found a fresh surprise awaiting. In short a letter thrust under the door; and this, taking to the light, I perceived to be addressed in a female and by no means inelegant writing.

'So ho,' I mused, 'Lady Dorothea, I wonder; or the duenna, Miss Harriet; yet why so soon?' But it was neither.

'Mr Sturrock,' it read, 'Sir; it has come to my ears that you are engaged with an enquiry concerning the late most lamentable death of Mr Robert Mytton the younger. Concerning this there is certain matters which I could acquaint you of, but only in the most private circumstances. It would be imprudent in me to call on you as I am Well Known and Recognized, and also improper, but if you can make it your pleasure to wait on me I shall be at home to receive at about four of the after noon tomorrow. Yrs in respect Mrs Margaret Huxey. (Lodging at 18, Bloomsbury Market, off Hyde Street.)'

'So ho,' I said again; for how could our Mrs Britannia know that I was about such enquiry when I had enjoined all who knew of it to strictest secrecy? In short, had Lady Dorothea or Miss Harriet blabbed, which I considered unlikely, or was some other person or persons already fearful of how close I was sniffing at their heels? I reflected on this over a pipe and a glass or two of Madeira before packing Master Maggsy off to bed, lest some of his jewels of observation should disturb me, and sitting down to pen a stylish reply as follows. 'Madam; I am much privileged by your most kind communication, yet somewhat perplexed as you fancy that I have any concern in the manner of Mr Robert Mytton's lamentable death. I am persuaded by all the appearances, and as very surely it will be brought in at the coroner's enquiry, that the unfortunate young gentleman died of his own hand. Nevertheless, dear madam, I cannot restrain my pleasure at waiting upon you as appointed about more agreeable business. Viz; to offer my devotion to your person and your Art, and in particular to your supreme portrayal of that Britannia who is the Soul of all our defiance to the Corsican Monster, Bonaparte. I subscribe myself, madam, ever yr most dvted svt, Jeremy Sturrock.'

There is few can pen a more genteel letter than me when I put my mind to it, as you must have remarked already my elegant but unaffected style, and I sat for a while satisfied with that before turning to deeper matters. I have set down everything most precisely for your consideration and being a lady or gentleman of near enough as good wit as my own—else you would not be reading this book; the which I pray you have purchased honestly and not merely borrowed or stolen—you will by now know as much as I did at this turn. So no doubt you will have seen through that trick of the locked door, the only way it could be done, thus perceiving that I had five or six interested parties from which to choose the villain or villains. But as to whether Mr Mytton was killed by a fond, jealous lover; removed as an obstacle by another pair of greedy hands snatching at Lady Dorothea's fortune; or murdered because he had caught a whiff of some dark ingenious plot, I had as yet but little light.

Nevertheless I was persuaded that we should see more when we had sorted out the sprats from the herrings in our other various matters; namely Polly Knapp's antics and Nell Ewer, the affairs of the man Boosey, that knife either at me or Holy Moses, and not least Mrs Britannia Huxey's billet doux. With which reflection I betook myself to bed; somewhat unsteady but not ill pleased, for I dearly love a teasing mystery.

CHAPTER FIVE

I arose with a touch of the livers but was somewhat improved by a considerable breakfast set up by my good house woman; a worthy, respectable crone who also serves as attendant to the excellent Mrs Spilsbury in her dispensary downstairs. So restored with a rump steak, a mutton pie, quince jelly and a quart of gingered ale, I retired to array myself for the inquest, stylish but sober as befits the occasion; but I had not yet finished setting my neckcloth to a nicety when Maggsy came to the door whispering, 'You got company,' and when I enquired who the damnation it was at this hour, he answered, 'That actor, the booby; and Mr Tom Cullen. Like as if they've come to a burying.'

Indeed there was a graveyard look about the pair when I went in to them, both standing in the window, each with his hat tucked in the crook of one arm and a cane under the other, and as solemn as mutes. Mr Cullen said nothing, and the other did a bow like a board being bent in half with a crack and announced, 'We have certain business with you, Mr Sturrock.'

I gazed at him with some disfavour and he bowed again. 'I am here on behalf of my principal, Mr Jack Dashwood, to present his card.' This he did, getting it out from somewhere, dropping his hat at the same time, scrabbling it up again while looking at Mr Cullen for support and continuing, 'In propriety, sir, I should hand this to your friend to arrange the formalities, but as Mr Dashwood does not know of your friend, sir, it was concluded to hand it to you. Also Mr Dashwood was of two minds whether to fight you honourably, as being yourself a person of inferior rank, or whether merely call upon and horsewhip you.'

I felt my neckcloth constricted and the blood rising to my head. 'What of God's Name are you talking about?'

At this Master Maggsy snickered, while Mr Nincompoop turned a look on him as if wondering what it was, which you could hardly blame him for, and said, 'In simple, sir, Mr Dashwood proposes a duel. If convenient to you, sir, he proposes Hyde Park Fields; with pistols.'

'With pistols?' I asked, somewhat strangulated. 'What is this? One of your fantastical Drury Lane burlesques?'

'No, sir,' Mr Cullen answered, speaking up for the first time. 'It ain't. I don't like it neither, it's a tomfool business, but yesterday you saw fit to insult poor Jack in the presence of Lady Dorothea Hookham and others. It's all over the town by now. Even last night, when Jack made his entrance, some lout in the gallery bawled "Hot coffee!", and within a minute they'd all taken it up. Damn it, Mr Sturrock, it could ruin him; he could be laughed off every stage in London. He's bound to call you out or be taken for a coward.'

'Better a coward than a corpse,' I retorted roundly. 'Don't you know I'm the best pistol shot in England?' In truth I had no proof of this as I had never taken the rest of 'em on, but it sounded well enough.

Lilley blenched at that but continued on his course like a ship heading for the rocks. 'That's as may be. But Mr Dashwood will have satisfied his honour.'

'Be damned to honour,' I said. 'He'll have very little honour left with a pistol ball rattling about inside his skull. And I don't hold with killing a man only because he's a bad actor. If we shot all the bad actors about London there wouldn't be a theatre left open in a fortnight.'

Maggsy snickered louder than ever and Mr Cullen looked as if he was sorely tempted to lay his cane about the little wretch's shoulders, but observed instead, 'You have a poor humour, Mr Sturrock. I dislike this talk of killing, and there's no need of it. Jack will be satisfied enough to wing you.'

'Begod,' I rejoined, 'that's uncommon kind of him; though I suppose he knows the surviving party of a fatal duel is charged with murder. Tell me now, is it true he's courting Lady Dorothea Hookham?'

Mr Cullen eyed me sharply. 'What's that to do with you?'

'It's the talk of Drury Lane. But he'll find it damnation difficult to pay his court from Newgate Gaol.'

'Mr Sturrock,' the other cried, near enough weeping with vexation, 'will you meet my man or not?'

'To be sure I'll meet him,' I promised. 'But answer me one thing first, Mr Lilley. The night Mr Mytton shot himself where was you and Mr Dashwood and Mr Cullen, about the time of Britannia subduing the waves?'

'What's this, sir?' Cullen demanded, sharper than ever. 'Was there some mischance about Bob Mytton's death?'

'Not if you don't call blowing his own head off a mischance. It's a simple matter. I'm ordered to the inquest, and our old fuzz-buzz of a coroner's as full of questions as an egg is of meat. I like to have the answers pat.'

'Dear God,' Mr Lilley wailed, distracted. 'Are we or are we not trying to arrange a duel?'

'And so you shall,' I assured him kindly. 'But tell me that first.'

'In the gentlemen's dressing room,' Cullen said, 'about a game of cards.'

'I'm particular partial to a hand of whist myself,' I observed. 'Was it whist?' He looked at me hard, but then nodded and I asked, 'So that's four of you. Who was the other man?'

He paused an instant on that, but replied, 'Digby.'

'So there we have it clear,' I said, yet recalling as Boosey had claimed that when he went to fetch these fine gentle-

63

men there was only Dashwood, Lilley and Mr Cullen present and wondering which was lying. 'It's of no account,' I finished. 'Now what was this about a duel?'

Lilley set to talking at a hand gallop to get it done with. 'My principal proposes nine o'clock tomorrow morning under the elms in Hyde Park Fields. He can procure a pair of excellent duelling pistols. Will that suit you?'

'No, bedamn, it won't,' I told him. 'We'll use my own holster pistols or nothing. A bit old fashioned now but they still throw true and they'll take an arm off as neat as a whistle. If your man's troubled about looking like a coffee pot he won't need to worry more, for it'll be a coffee pot without a spout.'

'I find your manner coarse and vulgar, sir,' he announced down his nose. 'But your own weapons so long as the seconds approve. And what of seconds, sir? You will be provided?'

'I shall be provided,' I promised. 'As comical seconds as you ever saw. Seconds to fit the occasion.'

'Damn it, Nick,' Mr Cullen cried, 'call it off. It'll be a farce.'

'I always knew you had the best sense, Mr Cullen,' I agreed warmly. 'A farce indeed. But let it be if Mr Dashwood's tired of having two arms. For now, Mr Lilley, there's another matter. The other night I was set upon by three fellows close by here. To be sure I routed 'em. It takes more than three drunken roisterers to put me down. But I know for certain that one rogue came from Drury Lane. Was that another farce d'you think, Mr Lilley?'

The fool turned from putty to pease pudding colour and back to whore's belly pink; a most unlovely sight. 'I do not know what you mean. As you said, sir, drunken roisterers. There's a deal too many of them in London. Lord, sir,' he protested, 'you hop from one thing to another like a flea on a bed pan. It sets a man's mind in a whirl.'

I forbore to tell him that such was my stratagem, but

said, 'So let it be; mere drunken roisterers. But if there was any fresh attack I should fancy it was set up by some person or persons having reason to be fearful of me. And my natural inquisitiveness might then lead me to find out why.' The warning was plain and Mr Lilley turned a shade towards pease pudding again, but this I affected not to notice and concluded, 'Now, Maggsy, take that grin off your face, and lead the gentlemen down the stairs.'

So I was left to muse on several curiosities, until Master Maggsy came back with a rush and scutter, announcing, 'God's Truth, you've done it this time, you can't keep out of trouble, can you? They mean to kill you one way or another; only thing is I never see a duel before, so that's something, but you're a deader for sure.'

'Be damned to your senseless chatter,' I told him. 'We've better things to think about than Drury Lane fantasticals. Be off about your business.' This being first to deliver my billet doux for Mrs Huxey, and then on to his lessons with Holy Moses and keep his ears sharp there. After that to the Brown Bear and engage in conversation with the serving wench with intent to discover whether she knew the rogues who first started tossling her, next to the Long Acre Tavern there to observe whether Holy Moses did indeed meet and confer with the man Boosey, and finally to wait on me as I should appear and to keep away from my Madeira else I'd have the skin off his back for it.

Thus I went about my own affairs, but I shall not weary you with a description of the inquest. Suffice it to say that I gave my testimony simple and clear, answering just what I was asked and no more, particularly withholding my own observations and opinions. I was more interested to observe the person of Mr Robert Mytton the elder; an iron visaged man, tight lipped, of over hung eyes, wearing his own grey hair, and sparse of his words as though they themselves were gold coins which he hesitated to fling down lightly. The sum of it was that he knew of no reason why his son should commit this dreadful act unless it be gaming losses, which was a failing of the younger Mr Mytton, a match was in contemplation with a lady of quality but had somewhat hung fire; and the fatal armament itself, though lying on the coroner's table clear for all to see was never so much as mentioned.

It is ever a wonder and mystery to me how people can be so deceived by mere appearances, but it was certain sure that our famous coroner had already made up his mind, and though with all manner of regrets, condolences, respects, etc., to the great banker his verdict was brought in as I desired and expected; namely self murder, or *felo de se*. This being accomplished I took myself off quickly to watch Mr Mytton come out; and by so doing observed yet another element in this deep mystery.

The carriage was already waiting, a town coach and pair of sober appearance but singular excellence and, as I perceived, with uncommonly stout springs; which struck me somewhat curious, for our banker although looking like iron did not otherwise have the appearance of a particular heavy man. A big hardy fellow of a coachman was seated on the box, where there was also a pair of pistol holsters mounted, and the footman standing alert at the door; likewise as hardy as his mate, but having a bilious pallor about his face and a wry twist of the lips as if suffering from a spasm of the belly. 'So ho,' I murmured, 'has Nell Ewer been already up to her tricks then?' but did not have time for more as on that instant our banker appeared, in no very pretty temper, and was shut in by this footman who then climbed up on the box moving stiff, again like a man with a gripe of the guts. Upon that the coachman whipped up at once and they clattered away to the corner, turning east; while I again observed, 'So ho.'

For my part I repaired to a nearby livery stables where they know me and hired a more modest hackney, though not without some trepidation at the expense, as I could not yet see any profit to myself in this business. However it was a damnation long walk from here to Cornhill, neither did I fancy taking one of the Bow Street horses for it; I ride a fair seat, but there are too many mischances which might startle these wayward and uncertain creatures in the City. Directing my driver I settled to watch the passing pageant and to reflect on our mystery; mostly the sick look on that footman's face and my own necessary stratagems.

Under a signboard which portrayed an industrious bee and the legend 'Mytton and Co. Bankers and Bullion Brokers', the office was of a meaner sort than I expected, close and dark inside with a high barrier or counter where there was a pimpled youth scratching importantly in a ledger.

To cut a long business short, being viewed by one clerk after another each more doleful than the last and growing somewhat choleric myself, in the end Mr Grabble was fetched; a little pinkish rascal behind steel rimmed spectacles tut-tutting and twitching his nose at me, not unlike the very gnomes or dwarfs that are supposed to dig out the gold and of some self importance by the look of him.

He was another I resolved on words with when occasion served, but for the present I offered Lady Dorothea's letter and after some further head shaking and muttering, mainly of Mr Mytton not being in the sweetest of tempers, more trotting to and fro and whispering, I was at length admitted to the Temple of Midas itself. A private cabinet of dark and solemn panelling with one close barred window, a heavy oaken door in the further wall, and a big table or desk with Mr Mytton himself seated behind it. The letter was lying before him and as I was brought in, like a poor criminal before his judge, he looked up at me from beneath Gothick eyebrows and uttered but one word, poking at the paper with his quill. 'Well?'

I can suit short words to short as well as any man and

I said, 'You have the sum of it there, sir.'

He regarded me with the iron hard gaze. 'You was at the inquest. Yet you said nothing of this.'

'I should not have been believed. You saw our coroner for yourself.'

Looking at the letter again he observed, 'By God I did. And Dorothea's no fool. I'll hear what you have to say. But be brief. I've work to do.'

Brief it was. I related the tale plain and simple, and when I concluded he announced, 'Seems you've a pair of eyes in your head.' I was most obliged to him for that, and bowed while he demanded, 'Who did it?'

'One or perhaps two of six certain people.'

'Then why don't you take 'em?'

Allowing myself a small slight fawning, such as it is always best to approach these bankers with, I explained that we did not yet know which villains to take, nor what conspiracy they was about and finished, 'Moreover there is a certain quandary. A verdict being issued the law is satisfied. The case is closed.'

'Is it?' he demanded. 'By God we'll see about that.'

Doing very well I smiled on him like one of his own clerks. 'But it'll need your hand in it, sir. A letter of complaint or instruction to the Bow Street magistrate commanding the attention of his best man.'

He gazed at me while you might count ten but then struck the desk a smart blow with a gavel or little mallet, and on the instant a clerk appeared. 'Letter,' Mr Mytton said, and the poor devil stumbled over his feet to seat himself at a high desk under the window and wait humbly. 'Take this,' the banker ordered. 'To the Magistrate, Bow Street. Sir; touching the death of Mr Robert Mytton. From certain fresh information now laid before me I am persuaded that the verdict of the Coroner's Court this day was a miscarriage. I conclude that Mr Robert Mytton was killed and murdered by some person or persons at present

68

unknown and desire to have this verdict reversed. To that end I require you to set on the man best suited of your force to investigate this matter to the bottom. This same man to use his best efforts and all attention with a view to the speedy apprehension of these person or persons.' He considered that for a time, added, 'Your obedient servant,' and said, 'Copy.'

The poor creature got himself out again and I was left in silence while Mr Mytton studied today's issue of *The London Packet*, a most excellent newsprint much affected by gentlemen of the City. So we remained, myself revolving several naughty and immoral thoughts which I shall not set down here for fear of offence, until that wretched clerk crept back to lay his letter before the master, who read it through and scratched his name at the bottom. This accomplished he pushed it across to me saying, 'That'll be your business done. Give you good day.'

With this document in my hands I could now permit myself to move more boldly; as you shall ever observe, dear ladies, that a piece of written paper may be used in many clever and various ways, not the least that with some slight stratagem I could begin to see a small profit to myself in it. But still with a very proper affectation of knowing my place I said, 'There are certain questions which I must put to you, sir.'

Mr Mytton gazed at me transfixed, while the clerk remained half out of the door as if he were struck into a pillar of salt. I myself was most concerned to see what kind of a seizure Mr Mytton would take, being of this iron grey colour and not the full blooded claret and port appearance of most gentlemen in the City. But he was spared to us and at last got out, 'By God, you're an impudent rogue.'

'With respect, sir,' I pronounced humbly, 'in your own admirable words, "To the speedy apprehension of these person or persons".'

Yet again there was a stricken silence until in a strangely

throttled voice Mr Mytton repeated, 'By God ...' and asked finally, 'Well, what is it you want?'

I was somewhat perturbed for the poor gentleman's health, and to soothe him answered, 'Very simple, sir. Have you heard of any of your household or your servants being took sick lately? Most likely a griping of the belly.'

So far from soothed, this time it was like an explosion of grape shot. 'God's Blood,' he roared, 'are you cracked, man? How do I know? What have I to do with my servants' guts?'

Now here is a curious circumstance. The door was set back in an alcove or recess in the thickness of the wall. From where Mr Mytton sat he could not see it, but I could; and I observed it open just a crack as softly as it had closed, observed also the glint of what could only be one eye of a pair of spectacles behind. Whether but for this I might have warned him that he had a suspected female poisoner in his household I still do not know; I was of two minds about it even then, being curious to see how this business would turn out, and with that Mr Grabble flapping his ears there caution seemed the better part of speech. I asked instead, 'Was Mr Mytton inclined to your profession, sir?'

It looked like another explosion, but at last he said, 'He was not. Had some notion of buying a commission in the Hussars.'

'So he was of a patriotic turn of mind?'

'Like most of 'em at his age. Told him often enough that in this war that's coming it's gold and iron'll win it not galloping about on a horse.'

'A very proper sentiment,' I agreed, watching the door and that bright shining eye of glass, concluding that Mr Grabble should have heard enough for one day, and adding softly, 'Your pardon, sir, but the door is a little open.'

'Grabble,' he remarked and roared of a sudden, 'Grabble, God damn you, shut that damned door and take yourself off.'

70

It closed incontinent, and I enquired, 'Does he do that regular?'

'Regular enough,' Mr Mytton grunted. 'Thinks I don't know, the fool. But I humour him so far. The man's useful, and he don't talk.'

As to that I was in some doubt but I said, 'Very likely, sir,' and then asked, 'Can you tell me what kind of bankers Isaacs and Fettelson are?'

'Expectation brokers.' He paused, gazing at me, and then as sudden exploded again. 'God's Blood, don't tell me that's what the puppy was about?'

'About what, sir?' I enquired.

'Expectations, you fool. Fettelson's advance money on the prospects of inheritance. Let some young rogue have an estate or fortune coming to him and he can raise hard cash on it in advance. By God, had I known Bob was up to that game I'd have had his liver out myself.'

Again fearful of Mr Mytton's health, for I should get no profit if he were taken of a seizure, I advised him, 'Pray be calm, sir. There's no such indication. Isaacs and Fettelson was only spoke of in passing. All the same,' I added, musing on it and upon Mr Dashwood, 'could an arrangement of that kind be made in prospect of marriage? To a considerable heiress?'

'It'd hang with the settlement. Fettelsons don't pay out on hopes. And that cock won't fight neither. I was prepared to make Bob a handsome allowance myself as soon as he come to terms.' Mr Mytton stopped again. 'God damn your eyes for an impudent rogue, what d'you mean? How d'you know so much?'

'I had the honour and privilege of calling on Lady Dorothea and she was very plain with me. A most uncommon and unusual lady. I formed the opinion, indeed, that she was of Whiggish or even Bonapartist turn of mind.'

'Fiddle-faddle,' he retorted. 'That's the fashion with

71

modish educated women these days. But the Hookhams are a true old Tory family. The only son, Lieutenant Lord Hookham killed in an engagement with the French off Antigua two years or so back, and the old man now somewhat stricken and waiting only to see an heir, a fine bouncing grandson, before he dies.'

'And what was Lady Dorothea's mind on that?' I asked, treading cautious.

'Why she dotes on the old man, for all her crackpot notions. If he wants an heir of the Hookham blood she'd do her best to get him one.'

'So,' I said, more cautious still, 'it would seem there was no hindrance or impediment to the marriage?'

Expecting another blast I waited for the grapeshot, but he answered mild enough, even with a touch of grief I fancied. 'Save only that rogue of mine was hanging fire. But he'd have come round to it. Begod he was coming.'

'Are you sure of that, sir?'

'Damnation,' he roared at me, 'don't a man know his own son?'

Reflecting that such was unlikely in these critical days I answered humbly, 'It is much to be hoped so. But two more questions, sir; both I fear somewhat delicate. In short, have you heard anything of a certain young woman, person, or actress of Drury Lane known as Miss Virginia Posset? And is the rumour or tale that you made some threat to disinherit your son correct?'

This produced a hard silence while you might have counted ten. Then in a somewhat throttled voice again he said, 'I've heard of the wench; she's most like a whore. But it's a poor man who'll deny his son a whore or two at that age. As to the other, the rogue twitted me with her, swearing that he'd marry her in despite of me if I didn't let him have his own way. To which I answered that if he did I'd see him damned on a guinea; or pack him off for a daily clerk to our new bank in the Barbados.'

'But that was near enough a jest, no doubt?'

'As near a jest as it can be when an obstinate young devil dares to bait his own father. Have you done now?' he asked. 'For I'll tell you plain, my man, I'm losing patience with you.'

'There's little else, sir,' I assured him, all humility once more. 'Only this. Did you ever hear any whisper or word from your son that he might have caught some hint of French intelligence at work? He was shot with a French made pistol.'

A man of quick intellect, despite his banker's manner, he got the drift of it fast enough. 'Bonapartist spies, eh? They say the place is swarming with 'em. No,' he mused, 'Bob never spoke of that. And I think he would, mind, for I've access to them who'd be most concerned. So you think that's it? The lad found himself on the track of something and got a bullet in his head to quieten him?'

'It might be; it'll bear thinking about. Or it might be a case of some other young gentleman with his eye on Lady Dorothea's fortune and providing an heir for the Hookham titles and estates. It might yet be something deeper still, but you can be assured we shall find out. And I'll not detain you longer now, sir.'

He sat gazing at me as if I was one of those new, rare and strange beasts exhibited in Mr Pidcock's Menagerie, announced 'You'd better not, by God; you're a damned insolent rogue as don't know his place,' struck the desk a blow with his gavel and bawled, 'Grabble!' When that worthy appeared he added, 'Take Mr Sturrock out; and the next time he comes give me good warning that he's here.'

The little gnome himself was of no very kind manner and he led me through the other clerks, all whispering and peering, till we reached the street. Bubbling and simmering there he got out, 'God's sake that was uncivil, sir, pointing to me at the door. How was I to know that you were not about some attack or robbery on Mr Mytton? It's been done before. I was but doing my duty to watch you.'

'Mr Grabble,' I said, 'let us not offend each other, for we've interests together as I shall tell you in a minute. But for now I'll observe that if any whisper was to get around as to the purpose of my visit here, or the contents of that letter Mr Mytton wrote, I might feel bound to warn him that there are people in this office who carry his business abroad. I can't guess what he'd answer, but you must know as well as I do that he ain't a man of nice temper.'

He sucked his chaps in at that, and I continued more benevolent, 'But now for the better part of it, Mr Grabble. I've heard as you're a particular smart man about money. Well then it so happens I've got a thousand or so lying idle and I'd like to see it put out to earn a profit. How d'you say? Would you fancy to advise me over a bottle of claret?'

It was a clever stroke to throw off on the instant, but I am never at a loss for a stratagem. The little rogue jigged about on his knees like a man straining not to piss himself for eagerness. 'You couldn't come to a better shop,' he announced. 'A thousand, you say. You can do very nice in the City with that.' Then he jerked his nose up at the signboard over our heads. 'But not with this lot. Keep clear of him, Mr Sturrock.'

'So ho,' I asked, 'is he in shoal water then?'

Mr Grabble laid his finger against his nose. 'A word to the wise. Too much at venture. He wants but one loss and he's hammered.' He nodded and winked at me. 'I can place you better than Mytton and Company. When d'you say, Mr Sturrock? I commonly repair to the Cornhill Coffee House between one and two of the clock.'

'Let it be tomorrow; or the day after,' I said, and so took myself off not without a chuckle or two at the simpleness of these little gold digging gnomes. Mr Grabble might serve a turn or tell me something more if I had need of it; or if not I could let him rest.

CHAPTER SIX

So much accomplished I debated whether I should then
return to Bow Street to report to my master but concluded
not lest Mr A. should have some different plans from my
own. You shall note that in the Art and Science of Detection it is always well to act with a proper respect of your
authority but still to arrange it that you are left to go about
the business in your own way. Thus I could now use Mr
Mytton's paper as and when I thought fit explaining if
the need arose that it had slipped my memory, being hot
on the scent, or even have old Abel Makepenny our clerk
lose it among his other documents. That decided I engaged myself another hackney and directed the man to
set me down at Mr Hackett's eating house: though not
without some misgiving at the cost as these surly rascals
all charge too much for their flea bitten service.

Somewhat to my surprise and more to my displeasure
Master Maggsy was awaiting me there, sitting on the step
in spite of his genteel pantaloons and coat, bandying in-
sults with two or three other urchins or street arabs and
spoiling to start a fight. But on my arrival he leapt to his
feet scattering these young imps like chaff—which I
assisted with my cane—and advanced with the light of his
two chiefest pleasures on his face; bloodshed and disorder.
'Knowed you'd come here,' he announced before I could
get a word in, and added with relish, 'God's Truth, you've
done it this time, you have; you've put the cat among the
pigeons with a vengeance. Old Holy Bones's gone and
bolted and nobody knows where; and that ain't the best of

75

it neither. Mother Knapp's got her throat cut. God's Whiskers, you're a terrible man for causing trouble, there's no end of it when you're about.'

I learned the full tale in Hackett's after a shoulder of salmon—not all that fresh, being every minute of two days out of the water—a beefsteak and oyster pie and a morsel or two of prime Cheshire, firmly forbidding Master Maggsy to let fall his jewels of the English language before we'd done with this, for there is no good ever comes of discussing throat cutting over a steak and oyster pie. But at last I leaned back, called for another quart of ale, and said, 'Now then; and start your report at the beginning, in due order,' this also being a good exercise for the young.

'Not a lot with Mrs Huxey,' he confessed, 'where I took your letter. Dunno whether that's a whore shop or not but there's a gaggle of females about, and a fair stink of scent and they got a little blackamoor dressed in a turban for a page boy; but genteel otherwise. This Mrs Huxey don't look so much when she ain't waving her fish fork about, but still plenty of her, and when I says "From Mr Sturrock" she says "Oh, the dear man", and wants to know if I'd fancy a cup of chocolate, so I says I'm game for anything once and then she starts asking a lot of questions about you.'

'You can pass over that,' I said, 'I've a fair idea of what they'd be.'

'That's right,' he agreed, 'it's certain sure somebody wants to know what you're up to. Anyhow I told her what I guessed you'd want me to say on account of never telling the truth yourself if you can help it. And I said you was particular well thought of by His Majesty the King, God bless him,' the little villain continued hurriedly, 'and very dainty with the females, a rare proper man with the ladies, and she does a kind of screech and a giggle and observes that I'm a forward toad and I come away. That's about all save when I was coming out of the house them two actors was agoing in; them as are laying to kill you tomorrow, all fol-de-rol with their beaver hats acock and their boots shining and their little walking canes.'

'Not much in that either,' I told him. 'It's plain they put the woman up to send for me. No sign of Mr Tom Cullen?' He shook his head, and I asked, 'What else?'

'Fine old sight in Holborn,' he volunteered. 'Couple of soldiers riding down and one of un's hoss reared and that set off a phaeton bolting into a carriage and pair and they turned against a brewer's dray and overset a couple of chairmen and a rare screeching old woman in their sedan; you never heard such a roaring and cussing and cracking of whips. Likewise I hadn't laughed so much since my old master, Mr William Makepeace the Practical Chimney Sweeper, made a go at a big fat cook's tits one day when we was aclearing a kitchen flue and she laid him cold with the rolling pin.'

'Be damned to your observations of London life,' I retorted. 'Come to Holy Moses now, and Mother Knapp.'

'Like I told you,' he answered sulkily, 'one's up and bolted and t'other's got herself gutted; leastways, her throat cut. Nothing in Holy Bones's lodging, all his books and papers gone, greatcoat and hat, and that old hour glass he used to work his sermons with when in the preaching trade. He always said he'd never be parted with that so I reckoned he hadn't been took but made off on his own.'

'You show the glimmerings of sense,' I commended him. 'Continue.'

'Asked one or two of them about there if they knowed where he'd got to, in particular the rag and bones woman who keeps the next room and she said she neither knowed nor cared on account of having better things to think about; this being poor Mrs Knapp getting done for in Cross Street out of Long Acre. So I says "God's Whiskers that's something for old Sturrock ..."' The villain caught

77

my eye and amended hastily, '"For Mr Sturrock to chew over with his dinner", and took myself off there. Wasn't nothing to see though,' he added. 'Watchman must've washed the blood away. Likewise they'd took the corpus off so I didn't get a sight of that neither.'

'Doubtless a cause of some grief and dismay to you,' I observed. 'But what did you glean?'

'Little enough. Seems she must've been done last night and most like on her way back from the Drury on account of her oranges lying scattered all about, but wasn't found till today morning owing to the fog and the watchmen not fancying putting their noses into Seven Dials; and can't say I blame 'em. Some old woman discovered her and run screeching for the parish constable who then fetched the coroner's officers. This old hunks was still telling the tale to a crowd gathered around and from what I could make out it looks like somebody come up behind in the fog and finished her off before she had time to utter a squeak. Seems she damn near got her head cut clean off. Like the King of France,' he added. 'Did you ever hear that song? Mr William Makepeace used to sing it when in a good humour; "King Louis was the King of France before the Revolution, he went and got his head cut off and spoiled his constitution ..."'

The wicked rascal caught my eye and stopped short, to continue more soberly, 'Went around to her lodging after that but there wasn't no better to be had there; nothing but the horriblest crew of old bags you ever saw all wailing and yellocking and the gin flowing pretty near as free as the tears. They didn't know what had become of Holy Bones neither and didn't much care.'

'Was the man Boosey present?' I asked.

He shook his head. 'Never a smell of him.'

'Maggsy,' I enquired not expecting a sensible answer, as indeed I did not get one, 'What dark devilment have we here?'

'Dunno,' the rogue answered, 'but I don't like it. It ain't genteel to start with, and if you ask me Mother Knapp won't be the last one to get her throat cut. Why don't you go and catch a highwayman or two? At least they're respectable and you get forty guineas a neck for 'em. You won't have no good out of this.'

I let his impudence pass, for I was deep in consideration, and at last pronounced, 'Well, Master Maggsy, we cannot say for sure that this latest wickedness has much part with the death of Mr Robert Mytton. But when we reflect on Mother Knapp setting the wench Nell Ewer into that household it is not improper to conclude that some part there might be. Moreover when we consider yet more the closeness of our man Boosey in the matter we may conclude further that he knows too much to do him good. But as to what he and certain other villains are about is still another question.'

The little wretch listened with every appearance of attention to these profound observations, though reaching out for the last morsel of cheese upon the table, and I finished, 'Now pay attention to your own instructions. The first that you will not venture alone into the Seven Dials again until we have this business done with. I've already expended a damnation deal of money on your clothes, food and education, and I'll not have it wasted by you also getting your throat cut to no good purpose. The second that Holy Moses must be found. So you will occupy yourself going about all the coach stations enquiring of the ostlers and such like to discover whether he took a coach or not. The old rascal's most likely gone to ground here in London, but we must make a start somewhere. After that you will come to wait for me outside Mrs Huxey's residence in Bloomsbury Market.'

So I was left alone and in some disquiet which I could not by now put down to a mere touch of livers. Such being the nature of my trade I have seen much of human wickedness especially among the lower sort—though the better kind and sometimes even the nobility can be most damnable rogues when the fancy takes them—but I have never yet met even the lowest villain in which there was not some trace of hope, as we are none of us born or made wholly bad; but in this business so far I could detect no spark of human kindness anywhere, and in particular a woman who takes to philosophy and politics is the very devil.

Sitting for a time to let the steak and oysters settle I debated whether to put out a general Hue and Cry after Boosey and perhaps even Holy Moses. This I concluded against at last as there was small chance of finding either once they heard the hunt was up, and we had bigger game afoot than the mere rascally killer of poor Polly Knapp; the old drab was born to a bad end. Moreover I had a most inordinate desire to discover the name and nature of this game myself; how it touched upon Mr Robert Mytton the younger and, as I was now beginning to suspect, Mr Robert Mytton the banker himself. There is little profit in frightening off the hares to catch a rat or two and so reflecting, with several other moral observations, I took myself about the next concern; namely, to wait upon our Britannia, or Mrs Huxey.

The house in Bloomsbury Market was a moderate place in brick of the modern style, pretty enough to look at but nothing like so solid as my own modest establishment in Soho Square, where the residences are of particular gentility being mostly built at one time for the nobility and gentry who have now moved out to more commodious areas. Its door was opened for me by the little blackamoor page boy, most fantastical dressed and lighting up his dark little face with a wide white grin; indeed I was so taken by the pretty rogue that I near enough gave him a ha'penny, but thought better of it in time. So I was led up a staircase hung with engravings of the theatrical profession—the

Divine Sarah and Mr Kemble, Mr Sheridan, etc.—to a door on the first floor facing front.

It was a very fair sitting room done in Chinese wallpaper, and you never saw such a profusion of frills and furbelows, ribbons and favours, playbills, invitations and little fancy mirrors; scented and perfumed as Maggsy had said and uncommonly warm from a big fire. Furnished in the French fashion, all gilt and spindles, not forgetting a day bed now considered indispensable to any lady of pretension keeping up to the mode, with our Britannia herself reclining on it attired likewise in the French style and scandalous. Hair done in the Greek manner, cross ribboned sandals, a near enough nothing chemise gown and, at the danger of bringing a blush to my more genteel lady readers' cheek, never a one of her copious charms which could not be seen or guessed at without overmuch exercise; well enough in Paris, no doubt, where anything may happen, but out of place in London. Nevertheless, seeing how the appointment was clearly to be conducted, I did my best bow and as she held out her hand to me kissed the tips of her fingers, thanking God that Master Maggsy was not here to observe the scene.

'Such gallantry to call, Mr Sturrock,' she cooed like a pouter pigeon.

'No, ma'am,' I denied stoutly, 'but rather most gracious and condescending of you to receive me.'

She gave me a smile that might have fetched the varnish off a coach door, asking, 'A dish of tea, Mr Sturrock?' saying to the little blackamoor, 'Tea, Baba,' and enquiring again, 'an enchanting little moppet, Mr Sturrock, is it not so? Yes?'

'Enchanting indeed, ma'am,' I agreed, 'yet nothing near so enchanting as yourself.'

'Ah, la, Mr Sturrock,' she cried. 'What a bold creature; so quick. I declare you'll have me blushing.' I considered in private that what would have her blushing would set the gilded cock on St Giles' steeple crowing, but prudently kept my counsel and she continued, 'But be seated, Mr Sturrock, do; bring a chair up. Let us be *intime*.' So with a fit of the Frenchies again I drew up one of the armchairs somewhat misdoubting whether it would bear my weight while she cooed again, 'Such a famous man, Mr Sturrock.'

'Fame, ma'am,' I observed, 'paying its respects at the shrine of beauty; or Mars at the altar of Venus.'

'Ah, la,' she cried again, 'such fancy speeches. What a dear monstrous forward rogue it is.' But on this her little blackamoor brought in the tea, a dish which I can take or not but would sooner leave, and she busied herself with the ceremony in a whirl of perfume and muslin while announcing, 'For once I am free, like a little bird. Tonight the play contrives without me, so we have no need of haste; and I dearly love a *tête-à-tête* with a proper man.'

'As to that, ma'am,' I answered, 'in the Thespian brotherhood no doubt some are proper and no doubt some are not. But as the ancient philosopher observes,' I added, not to be outdone in the foreigns and very near as good as Holy Moses, ' "*Quod exitus ipsos tinctus felis*", as being translated to the vulgar means "You can't tell the colour of the cat till you let it out of the bag".'

She gave a silvery laugh which set the glass pretty bits on the mantelpiece tinkling in sympathy. 'And a droll, I do declare; a naughty witty creature.' But on that the foolery was over and she came straight at the business. She said, 'Yet we must be serious. Tell me now, there's a dear man, what d'you make of this most awful death of poor Mr Robert Mytton?'

'Why, ma'am,' I replied, 'there's only one thing you can make. The same as our jury brought in today. Self murder.'

She let out a little screech and clapped one hand to her tits. 'Ah the poor soul; and all for love. But do you believe that?'

'Well, ma'am,' I answered, 'I understand love's a disease much like the vapours or fever; it takes different people different ways.'

This time she gave me a slap on the knee which damned near put the joint out. 'Naughty creature. I did not mean that. I mean do you truly believe Mr Mytton did this dreadful thing?'

'I believe what my own eyes tell me, ma'am.'

She gave me an uncommonly keen look despite the simper with it. 'But that odious fellow Boosey will have it that you questioned him most closely.'

'Boosey?' I enquired, affecting innocence.

'The flunkey. And a most rude, vulgar and disobliging man it is.'

'They commonly are,' I observed. 'Flunkeys, chairmen, coachmen and post boys is always the surliest dogs ever. No doubt God had some inscrutable design in creating 'em though I never discovered what it was. But I recollect the rascal now, and a more suspicious looking rogue I never saw. Yet that's the nature of flunkeys too and no doubt he's as honest as most. He's of no matter. Indeed I've heard he's left the Lane; and devilish uncivil to poor Mr Knyvet in the manner of his going. Where's he off to, do you know?'

'Why,' she answered, falling into it like a simple lamb, 'to be a coach footman, so they say.'

I contrived a lecherous sigh and asked, 'With so much beauty spread before me what account is Boosey? Yet I wonder who'd have that surly rogue for a footman?'

'La,' the woman whispered, heaving like an earthquake, 'you're a wicked rogue yourself, Mr Sturrock. You'd talk an innocent girl into trouble, you would. I neither know nor care who's took the wretch on. Bless me,' she added, 'but you're a bashful man for all your gallant speeches and you'd think me a very tigress the way you keep so offish.'

83

The shameless wanton edged back a bit on the sofa, and I confessed, 'No, ma'am, far from bashful I'm a man as must restrain himself, and particular partial to a warm ripeness in a lady. But it would be ungenteel in me to presume on such short acquaintance. Pray let's talk of less temptatious things; a mere gossip. Where did you hear that Boosey was going for a footman?'

'Fiddlesticks to Boosey,' she cried. 'If it's any matter to you I fancy it was Jack Dashwood as told me. Give over teasing, Mr Sturrock.'

With that she got her arms about my neck in a regular half-nelson, dragging me out of the chair, damned close to smothering me and near enough over-setting the sofa. It was touch and go, for the wild creature had the strength of ten while by sundry symptoms she was doing her best to bite off my left ear before proceeding to sterner diversions; but managing to get out, 'By God, for your own sake, ma'am, don't encourage me to tease,' I fetched her a slap upon the rump which might have felled a dray horse. Yet even this was no more to her than a mere amorous frolic, and she released what was left of my ear long enough to whisper in it, 'I adore a strong, impetuous man,' and then set about trying to get my coat down over my shoulders, somewhat disarranging my neckcloth.

I was close to losing patience, and saying, 'Then you shall see one, ma'am,' I employed a sweet little trick taught me by the Black Tinman; who, now being a champion pugilist with whom I sometimes take a practise round or two, had worked his way up through the Cornish wrestling. I shall not disclose its nature for it is seldom necessary to use it with more genteel ladies, but it steadied Mistress Britannia and we broke apart; she gazing at me somewhat stormily, opening her mouth to screech, and me patting her hams and saying, 'Let be, ma'am. You're an uncommon fine woman and no doubt a rollick with you'd be like a romp in a flower garden.'

'You spurn me,' she cried.

'Indeed no, ma'am,' I answered. 'I'd never be so churlish as to spurn such beauty. But I'm a man as likes to take his citadel by siege rather than by storm.'

Thus encouraged her bosom stopped its heaving, now resembling less of an earthquake and more like a mere pair of whales gambolling. You shall observe that such an encounter is not of necessity a part of the Art and Science of Detection, but you should be prepared for it if the occasion arises, as you should be prepared for anything. But your investigation must come first and, setting my neckcloth in order with some thankfulness again that Master Maggsy was not present, I concluded, 'I can think of no more rollicking nor felicitatious engagement in due time, ma'am; but for this present I'm about an enquiry.'

The stormy billows were stopped at once, likewise the tears. She gazed at me with no simpers about it this time. 'What enquiry?'

'I'll tell you plain in a minute,' I promised. 'But first a simple question or two. In short, what are you up to?'

'You're a proper man,' she countered. 'And I'm a warm woman.' But then, fiddling with the ribbons of her bodice, she turned down her eyelashes and confessed, 'I'll not have you shoot Jack Dashwood.'

'So ho,' I said. 'That's the way the wind sits.'

Mrs Huxey cast down her eyes again. 'I thought to sweeten you out of it. And I could ha' done. In thirty years on the boards I've softened many a harder man than you.'

'Begod, Mrs Huxey,' I cried generously. 'There's never a doubt of that. It would be a hard rogue who'd refuse you anything. But what's Mr Dashwood to you?'

She turned somewhat coy on that and I protested, 'Come, ma'am, we're talking plain; we're good friends. When there's leisure for it I could hope to be better. But if you're set against me shooting Dashwood I'm bound to ask why.'

'It was a monstrous wicked thing you said of him,' she

announced. 'Once let that cry of "Hot coffee" get around the galleries and poor Jack may whistle for his living. Have you ever known how cruel is the public?' She stopped again and then added, 'If you mean to know, he's my son.'

I gazed at her amazed, saying at last, 'Lord, ma'am, I wouldn't have thought you had the age for it. You must've been a mere girl at the time.'

'I was indeed,' she sighed. 'And simple in the bargain. A little silly chit in a band of strolling players. His father's a person of estate and shipping interest in Bristol. You'd be surprised if I told you his name; which I'll not do. But Jack's a gentleman born.'

'Anybody can see it,' I agreed. 'And I'll not press you further. But if it'll ease your mind I don't want to shoot the boy and it won't pay me to neither.'

'Then you'll ask his pardon and call it off?' she demanded eagerly.

But I shook my head on that. 'Pardon's a big word and I've my own face to think of. Yet the half of these duels are nothing but a bang and a miss. I'll engage that Mr Dashwood has no harm from me so long as he engages likewise. You take my meaning?'

She nodded in her turn. 'I take your meaning, Mr Sturrock; and I'll see to it.'

'You're a woman after my own heart in every possible particular,' I told her. 'But I'm a simple creature and there's one thing I don't have clear. Mr Dashwood's seconds only called upon me this morning. Yet you sent me your most genteel epistle last night.'

'They was talking of the duel in the theatre,' she answered, 'and I made up my mind on the instant.'

'It must have been uncommon instant,' I mused, 'such a bold and daring plan. And you wrote of matters concerning the death of Mr Mytton.'

'I thought that the surest way to fetch you.'

'But why should you fancy I had so much interest?' Seeing that the transports was safely over I sat myself close on the edge of the sofa. 'Come now, Mrs Huxey, my dear—and a dear inviting soul it is, I can scarce keep myself away—who wants to discover what I'm after at the Lane? Is it Boosey?'

'That odious creature?' she cried. 'La, Mr Sturrock, you're teasing again. If you will know, it was Polly Knapp. Polly works me a little favour now and again and it seemed a small thing to do for her in return.'

I considered privately that it was more like Polly Knapp knew how Mr Jack Dashwood stood to this over generous creature and made use of it accordingly, but said nothing; neither did I disclose that poor Polly was now lying quiet in St Giles parish mortuary, not wishing to find a screeching fit on my hands. Instead I mused again, 'Now here's a comical thing. I don't have the smallest concern with Mr Mytton's death, yet Polly Knapp seems anxious lest I might. I wonder could it be on account of some question I asked her by chance? About some wench she's lately put into service? A certain Nell Ewer.'

'That's the very thing,' our Britannia admitted. 'Not the name, as I never heard it before, but Polly spoke of a new girl and said I was to be sure and find out what you was after concerning her.'

'Why nothing,' I told the sweet creature. 'We all know Mother Knapp's naughty trade, but I've got bigger fish to fry. So now we have it clear,' I continued. 'You sent me your enchanting billet doux in obedience to Polly Knapp and then hearing later of Mr Jack Dashwood's duel you resolved to wrestle with me in his favour. Thus striking down two birds with one shot; an art I often practise myself. Begod, ma'am,' I declared, 'it does credit to your nature. You're a garden of temptation and I must tear myself away before I fall into it.'

'Pretty speeches again,' the saucy creature observed, 'but

if the truth's told, Mr Sturrock, you're more wind than blow.'

'Only let me have this business over,' I promised, 'and you shall find out what a blow it can be.'

'La, there's naughty,' she cried, but then asked shrewdly, 'What is this business, Mr Sturrock?'

There was a fine round answer to that which might yet be true; and also serving to explain my curiosity. 'Touching affairs of our Sovereign Lord the King, ma'am; and the safety of His Realm. To be plain it's suspected that we have somewhere a nest of Frenchy spies, and some of them frequent the Lane as there they can meet gentlemen from the Horse Guards and the Admiralty.'

She let out a little screech, clapping both hands to her tits as if she half expected an army of these rascally Frenchmen to fall upon her and ravish 'em. 'La, Mr Sturrock, what a fearful thing. And at our theatre, you say?'

'So it's thought; though I shall press you to keep that a close secret. It's a dark business, but when the tale comes to be told you shall hear it first; that I promise. Now, ma'am,' I added, 'there's only one more thing. I'd dearly like a word or two with Miss Virginia Posset. Where can she be found?'

'Ginny?' Mrs Huxey demanded. 'What can you want with that child?'

'Why, little enough,' I confessed. 'Merely that my young amanuensis or clerk was much taken with her at the Lane that other night. He's a sweet romantical lad and it'll please him to hear that I've passed on to her his admiration.'

The lady delivered a most ungenteel sniff, but said, 'Well, it's simple enough. The girl lodges here. I'll have Baba bring her.'

I shall be short with Miss Virginia Posset as she was of no importance; a little fanciful piece of watered milk and roses such as I could see no man doing murder for; unless

88

it was herself. Inside a minute or two I had the creature chattering like a magpie, though with little more sense than that flirtatious bird; an April shower of tears that Mr Mytton should so rashly shoot himself for love of her and, for what they was worth, two items concerning Mr Digby. The first that on the fatal night he was watching Miss Posset as an attendant nymph from the stage wings, but left that position on the fanfare of cannons and trumpets—thus, I reflected, giving him time to arrive in the passage by a different way a bit before I did myself—and the second that Miss Posset now supposed she would take him after all as, although having been somewhat straitened before, he was expecting to better himself with a legacy before long.

So one way or another I had garnered a little more, and at last I rose to take my leave not without several further pretty speeches, etc., to Mrs Huxey.

CHAPTER SEVEN

You may judge of my displeasure when I discovered Master Maggsy not waiting in the street as I had commanded but lurking with the little blackamoor by Mrs Huxey's door on the landing, and both with such looks of angel innocence as left no doubt of what they'd been doing. Not wishing to have an ungenteel scene about my exit I overlooked the one, though sorely tempted to give him a cut with my cane, and even took my own rogue down the stairs before demanding what in damnation he was at, listening at the keyhole for sure and was he looking for a lively thrashing to mend his manners?

'Watching out for you, that's what,' Maggsy answered stoutly, 'in case of any mischief. I keep atelling you somebody's going to cut your tripes out before you've done, and I see a couple of ugly looking villains through the window down there in the area kitchen, and I says to myself there he is in trouble again if he ain't careful.'

'Footmen,' I told him testily, though somewhat touched by the child's concern. 'Commonplace enough in a houseful of ladies.'

'Ain't nothing commonplace about this lot,' he replied. 'They looked more like bashers to me, and I see this sort of thing done before. I recollect once there was another chimney sweeper and his mates laying for Mr William Makepeace on account of under pricing the job, so they got a doxy to ask him up for a rollick; and when he was well about it they set to and beat the daylights out of him as he was took at a disadvantage with his britches down;

a very nasty situation. Mr William Makepeace reckoned he wasn't agoing to do no more rollicking for the rest of his days; but he did of course, him being another who couldn't let it alone.'

'Maggsy,' I promised, leading the monster away by the scruff of his neck, 'God and me sparing you, which grows hourly of greater doubt, some day you shall put your bawdy recollections down in a book where they'll be kept quiet; but for this present come to Holy Moses. Did you find any sign of him?'

'Very nearly wore my feet down flat,' he grumbled. 'Traipsed all round the coach houses; Bell Savage, Bull and Gate, White Bear and the lot but never a smell of him. He ain't took a coach nowhere, that's certain. Only thing I come upon was an ostler in a tavern by Holborn who says somebody like him stopped for a pennorth of gin just after light this morning; in a right fluster and went off heading east towards Smithfield.'

'There's little good of that,' I mused. 'If he's gone to earth there we might never find the old rascal. So we must let him rest for now; we've better business on hand. We'll go to find our learned Dr Blossum in Grub Street.'

So discovering a hackney we set out once more, though not without argument, as the surly rogue of a driver was unwilling to venture into those unsalubrious precincts with the night thickening into fog again. After some cursing and near enough a collision or two, for the traffic in London grows worse every day and even more hazardous in this weather, we at length reached Cheapside where our reluctant charioteer refused flatly to go further and I dismissed him with a blessing which surprised him and gave Maggsy a fit of the hiccups. Such are the perils of travel in our modern age.

This Grub Street, the lair of that miserable tribe of poor scribblers scratching out their living at a ha'penny a line, might well be the very Avernus of which Holy Moses is so apt to talk; only different from the Seven Dials in that most of these poor souls here are of too mild a nature or too cowed by their publishers to indulge in more desperate villainy. A short lane of close tenements lost in the fog, save where one or two miserable bookshops cast a feeble candlelight into the darkness; a few dim figures shuffling into the gloom, all hunch backed from crouching so long over their writing desks, and in those same bookshops a few more peering down their noses into musty volumes. We enquired in one of these for the whereabouts of one Dr Blossum, and I could not but reflect how profoundly did the immortal Doctor Samuel Johnson observe that no place affords a more striking conviction of the vanity of human hopes than a library.

We found our way at last to a dark entrance, groping up one flight of creaking stairs after another, and here indeed was one of the tribe in his den. It looked as if old Holy Moses made a better trade of screeving for he at least could most times afford a handful of fire whereas this place was as cold as a whore's love. A sloping roofed garret and one small window which let as much of the fog in as it kept out, an uneven board floor and a wooden bed in one corner, a litter of dog-eared books, dusty news sheets— and some of them in French as I was quick to perceive for though I do not speak the gibberish I know what it looks like—and Dr Blossum himself; dressed in a woollen night cap, topcoat and mittens and seated at a tall desk between two stinking candles and scribbling away with a quill for dear life. 'Well,' I thought, 'if this be a scribbler's lot God send me a good hanging,' but said, 'Dr Blossum, sir, my respects. You'll pardon our intrusion on your learned labours, but we met at Lady Dorothea Hookham's salon the other day.'

He peered at us from between the candles and in the prevailing gloom it was a wonder he could see us at all. 'You come from Lady Dorothea?' he asked, and then added, 'No, by God, the thieftaker. Don't like thieftakers,' he announced. 'Hang a man for forty guineas. Not that I wouldn't hang one for twenty at this present if you put the money straight into my hand. What d'you want?'

Maintaining my respect, as befits when consorting with philosophers, I replied, 'To be plain, sir, I'm engaged about an uncommon deep and devious conspiracy, and I'm persuaded you might help with my enquiry. But might I first ask what work you're on there? I've a mind for philosophy myself when I've time for it.'

'Philosophy?' he asked, taking a spoonful of snuff from the horn by his side, sneezing a cloud of it at us and damned near blowing the candles out, 'Then you're cracked. Philosophy never got any man a full belly. Here,' he continued, 'See for yourself,' and routed among his papers to thrust a sheet at me.

I bent closer to the light to examine it and read, 'Reflections on the Late Revolution in France, Together with Considerations on the Abolition of Monarchy, inscribed to that Most Excellent Patroness of Science, Philosophy, and the Arts, Lady Dorothea Hookham, by her humble servant Ezekiel Blossum, M.A., Ph.D., etc.'

'Observations from Plato, Suetonius, Seneca, Juvenal, Rousseau, Beaumarchais and a hundred others,' he said. 'The whole damned rag bag.' He was peering as well as he could see him at Maggsy and demanded, 'Who's he?'

'My clerk and servant, one Maggsy,' I explained.

'Don't look like a clerk to me,' the doctor announced. 'Looks like a regular rogue. And so do you for that matter. Dr Sturrock indeed! Not but that wasn't a monstrous fine observation you made on Dashwood. I split me sides with it.'

Somewhat nettled and profoundly shocked by this scandalous scribbling I retorted, 'We'll come to Mr Dashwood in a minute. But for now I'll say there are rogues and rogues. And I've rarely seen a prettier piece of roguery

93

than this,' flapping the paper at him. 'Treason and sedition, if you ask me, sir. And this.' I slapped one of the newsprints with my cane. '*Le Moniteur Universel*, the official newspaper of the French Government. What's that doing in an honest Englishman's lodging?'

'Why, you zany,' he cried, 'you can find it all over London. Lady Dorothea herself reads it.'

'I don't doubt that,' I said, soft and terrible, 'the lady being of a Bonapartist mind.'

'What of damnation are you driving at?' he demanded.

Judging that frontal assault would come best with this fellow I told him roundly. 'Frenchy spies. There's a stink of French spies about; and you and Lady Dorothea are a part of it.'

He gazed at me while you might have counted ten and then burst into a great guffaw which made the candles gutter. 'Lady Dorothea,' he wheezed, 'God's Teeth, that's rich. She'd have a fit. Why, you blockhead, that's just her fancy for want of better things to think about. The poor woman's husband hungry; got her mind stuffed with notions in need of something more useful in her belly. Though,' he added thoughtfully, 'it'll be the end of me when she gets it.'

'Blockhead yourself,' I returned. 'But what of this?' flipping the paper under his nose.

He gazed at me again in pity. 'God help us, but you're simple. Do but pay me a pension of one guinea a week while I'm about it and I'll write another to prove the opposite. "Reflections on the French Regicides",' he quoted, '"and their Inevitable Downfall at the Hands of Divine Justice and the English People". Compiled with observations from Plato, Suetonius, Seneca, Cato, Juvenal and all the rest of that same damnation rag bag. Come to consider,' he mused, 'that don't sound half bad. I suppose you don't know anybody as'd take it up?'

Seeing that he'd talk easier if he saw some chance of

profit in it I said, 'At a guinea a week I might think about it myself. For they're my sentiments.'

'Then by God,' he cried, 'I'm your man. And a fine learned work I'll promise you. How soon can we set about a contract? Take a pinch of snuff.'

'For the moment I've other business,' I answered hastily, 'though we'll consider it, depend on that. But for now, let's come to Mr Dashwood. It was you put the tale of the coffee pot about?'

To my relief he forgot his learned work and chuckled once more. 'A damnably monstrous fine observation. To be sure it was me. By God I'll have him laughed off every stage in London before I've done. I'd like to see that strutting cockerel at a public hanging in the first part.'

'In what way has he harmed you?' I enquired.

'In what way?' Dr Blossum cried. 'Why he tells my lady that I'm an old impostor. He ain't sure of her yet, but he'll get her now Bob Mytton's gone and there's an end of my dinners at Hanover Square when he does. Even a writer has to eat and with the price of everything going up I'm at my wits' end already. Shall we settle on a guinea a week? I'd write a damned fine book for it. Take a pinch of snuff.'

Fearing that I had spoken a trifle over hastily about that, I stuck doggedly to Mr Dashwood and announced, 'If you mislike the fellow as much as all that, Dr Blossum, I've excellent good news for you. I'm engaged to fight a duel with him tomorrow.'

'A duel?' he echoed.

'With pistols. At nine of the clock in Hyde Park Fields by Park Lane. And as of this I'm without a second. Now I wonder would you care to act for me?'

'As a second?' He thrust the feather of the quill into his ear as if to dust the snuff out of it. 'Well I dunno what a second does and I'm no hand with pistols, but if you mean to kill Dashwood I'm your man.'

'It's a long walk from here to Park Lane,' I said cautiously,

95

for I could not contemplate the expense of a carriage for him.

'Pooh,' he answered sturdily, 'I trudge to Hanover Square three times a week for my dinner.'

'Then I've a happier solution. You shall walk to my lodgings above Mrs Spilsbury's Dispensary in Soho Square. Be there at eight of the clock to take breakfast with me, and we'll have a hackney for the rest.'

'And I'm damnation obliged to you, Mr Sturrock,' he cried. 'Begod I'd walk from here to Bath to see Dashwood put down.'

'And so you shall,' I promised, though reflecting not in a duel for that would cost me too dear. 'If so be you'll answer me a few questions.'

'What questions?' he asked. 'Don't let's have no more of this Frenchy spies tarradiddle. That's mere pissing in the river.'

Master Maggsy, who so far had been sitting quiet, chose to snicker at this, being a coarse observation after his own heart, and I admonished him sharply before turning back to our Dr Blossum. I resolved on the truth; with favours in hand and hopes of more to come the poor simple soul would now speak plain enough to me and keep his mouth shut elsewhere. 'We still don't know,' I said. 'But we've a dark business here, and before I tell you what it is I shall swear you to silence. I wouldn't like to talk about a guinea a week to a man who can't keep his tongue still.'

'Depend upon it,' he cried. 'Never a breath out of me.'

'Very well then. Did you know that Mr Robert Mytton did not kill himself but was shot by another?'

He looked at me with a sort of pity. 'Any fool'd see that. I've spent the last two days considering what profit I could make of knowing, but concluded it might be too damned dangerous.'

'What?' I demanded, amazed. 'How did you find out?'

'First thing it didn't look right. Another, Robert Mytton

96

was never the sort to do such a tomfool act. And for the last I spoke to him in the Mutton Walk not half an hour before and he was in no mood for it neither. He was in a right royal rage.'

'So ho,' I said. 'Now we're moving somewhere. Continue.'

'Couldn't stomach no more of that play and went in there to find Grabble the banker's drudge. A pestilential tedious old fool but he'll share a bottle with anybody who'll listen to him talking. Well then, he was there somewhat whey faced with Mr Mytton just about turning away. So I say, "What now, Mr Mytton, don't you like the play neither?" and he answers, "Be damned to the play; I've got more business with a damnation pair of fine rogues."'

'We're doing business, Dr Blossum,' I announced. 'What else?'

'Why, little enough. The flunkey comes in then and says something to him. So far as I could catch it, that the ladies' room'd be best as they wouldn't be down off the stage for another twenty minutes yet. Upon which Mr Mytton took up the bottle of claret he'd got and a glass and followed the flunkey out.'

'So that's it,' Maggsy observed. 'Like you reckoned all along. Boosey done it.'

I admonished him to be seen and not heard and asked, 'Did you have any word with Mr Grabble?'

'Hardly to call it a word. He was tongue tied for a wonder. Says only that it was the most fartatious wearisome play he's ever seen and he's going home to his bed, and takes himself off.'

'But when he does talk, what's it about?'

The old fellow peered at me in the candle light. 'What d'you think? Had hopes of him at one time of a proposal to put up to his master. "Observations of the Wealth of Nations and how it is Increased by the Present Banking Systems". But nothing came of it.'

I was growing weary of his books, but these pitiful

scribblers are all the same; they fancy the whole world's as concerned with their direful scrivenings as they are themselves. 'Does he talk about his master's business? Mr Robert Mytton the elder?'

'Damned near nothing else. I don't listen to the half of it. Stocks and brokerage and banking and shipments of gold. For, mark you, where he is in the City he's but a minnow among the pikes and when he comes to the Lane he likes to put it t'other way about.'

'Shipments of gold?' I asked. 'From abroad?'

'Not as I know of,' Dr Blossum replied. 'Seems they call it a shipment even when they send it by coach.'

'And Mr Robert Mytton does that from time to time?'

'According to Grabble. Something about backing his paper with metal; some such nonsense. I told you, I don't listen all that much.'

'But where do they send it? Did you ever hear Mr Grabble speak of a bank in the Indies?'

'Spoke of little else for last weeks. Reckons Mytton's are over extended, whatever that means. And full of fearfulness about the dangers of taking gold by sea with the Frenchies and so many privateers about.'

The good doctor himself was speaking somewhat impatiently as if in haste to be rid of us and, to tell the truth, the cold of that garret and the stink of the fog and the tallow dips was getting into my own bones. I said, 'I'm deeply obliged, Dr Blossum, and I'll not detain you longer.'

'Just as well,' he answered, 'if you ain't inclined to talk about that guinea a week; though it'd be money well spent for the book I could present you with. We're wasting good candle grease in idle chatter and I'm engaged to finish this here as quick as may be. Lady Dorothea's to pay me ten guineas when I deliver it and that can't be too soon. I suppose you couldn't stop her marrying this Dashwood?'

'With but a dozen well chosen words.'

'Then, by God,' he demanded, 'what're you waiting for?'

He paused with the snuff spoon halfway up to his nose. 'Did he kill Bob Mytton?'

'I'll not yet commit myself on that. But if he didn't he's uncommonly close to them as did.' There concluding not to ask any further questions, for I was now starting to perceive what might be the truth yet needed time to reflect on it, I finished, 'So we'll give you good night now, Dr Blossum; until eight tomorrow for breakfast. A pound or so of steak and a veal pie or two. Together with a tasty Double Gloucester cheese, a touch of country made quince jelly and a quart of gingered ale to keep the cold out.'

Even in that miserable light I could see the poor soul's eyes gleaming between the candles. 'I suppose you couldn't make it seven o'clock so we don't have to hurry ourselves?' he asked.

'Seven o'clock it shall be,' I said, signalling to Maggsy who was still sitting silent.

'And I hope to God this Dashwood don't kill you instead,' the learned doctor finished. 'It'd be like my fortune to have you done for when you're considering a guinea a week for a damned fine book.'

'There's little doubt of the issue,' I assured him; as indeed there was not for I had my own plans.

So, somewhat saddened by the poor soul's plight and repenting my impetuosity in that easy promise which seemed to have taken such a sad grip on him, we felt our way down the stairs and out into the stinking fog again. A veritable pit of darkness, never a hackney to be seen, only a few poor lost souls of scribblers edging past us like unhappy wraiths, and scarce a glimmer of light until we groped ourselves into Cheapside and so by St Paul's. There is little to say of that Cimmerian noctambulation save curses, nor shall I offend you with Master Maggsy's improving reflections until we found our way at last to Fleet Street and a convenient eating house; not of the best sort but like a haven on this pestilential night. Here we restored

99

ourselves with a very fair dish of stewed eels and thus refreshed I pronounced, 'We now begin to see a certain light; in short, the substance of a plot which would contain all our observations so far and most of the several villainies we have witnessed.'

'Well it ain't Frenchy spies, that's for sure,' Maggsy said, 'for that old doctor'd be better off if it was; they say this Bonaparte gives out gold by the bucketful and I didn't notice no buckets of gold about. I'm grieved of that, as I never see one,' he continued, 'but I reckon you got to give up that notion.'

'I fear we must,' I agreed, in a high good humour. 'But only as we've an explanation now that fits better. An explanation to take in chatterbox Mr Grabble and Nell Ewer also known as Antimony Nell, a servant wench that gets herself killed with a broken head, a coach with uncommon heavy springs, a footman suffering the collywobbles and our Mr Boosey going for a footman himself. It's as pretty a bit of scheming devilment as ever I've seen, and I can even start to smell some reward in it. But we've much to find out still, so we'll take ourselves next to Ned's Coffee House by Drury Lane; where you yourself, Master Maggsy, discovered that Mr Digby may sometimes be met after the play.'

This we set off about now and, as I had planned it, by the time we reached the theatre people were turning out; a bustle of carriages and chairs, coachmen and grooms with torch boys lighting through the murk, and a medley of cries, curses and whistles. This coffee house itself is one of the more modish sort and much frequented by wits, critical gentlemen, actors and sometimes even Mr Sheridan himself, where country people visiting London will often repair to view the famous and listen to their elegant conversation. Yet I myself have never seen or heard anything all that remarkable here.

Tonight it was less attended than usual, for the wisest

parrots rarely chatter in a fog, and I began to have some fears for our errand until I spied Mr Digby at last and, somewhat to my surprise, Mr Tom Cullen with him. Both smoking their pipes they were sitting in a kind of ingle or nook with high backed seats, their heads close together in earnest talk, and one drawing lines and marks on the table top while the other watched and nodded from time to time.

They had neither perceived us, and drawing Maggsy back I gave him a few brief instructions, which he took quick and ready always being alert for mischief, and then slipped away to settle himself behind their pew; the little rogue can be as silent and near enough as invisible as a cat when he chooses, no doubt the training Mr William Makepeace gave him in thievery. For my part I exchanged a few words with the serving man, a good fellow who knows me well and with more sense than to interfere in my business, waited a minute or so to give Maggsy time to pick up what he could, and at length approached their table myself. 'Good evening, gentlemen,' I wished them, 'and well met. I was looking for you.'

They jerked apart sharpish, and Mr Cullen looked up at me a thought ill favoured, though still polite enough. 'Well met if you like, Mr Sturrock,' he answered, 'but damned irregular in view of our business tomorrow. And you're late to call it off if that's what you're thinking of. The gods howled "Hot coffee" at poor Jack again tonight.'

'A discomposing circumstance,' I agreed, 'and we must do our best to accommodate Mr Dashwood. But I've no wish to shoot him; unless he's set on it himself.' I turned to Mr Digby. 'We haven't had the pleasure of a conversation yet, sir, but I'll ask a favour of you. At this present I've only one second for tomorrow and I understand the affair needs two. Will you be good enough to act for me?'

He was, as others had observed, a dark visaged fellow, bony in the face, with uncommon hard eyes and mouth but now plainly taken aback. 'I don't know you, sir,' he observed, then looking at the other and asking, 'What d'you think, Mr Cullen? Is it in order?'

'Order enough,' Cullen replied. 'I've no objection, nor will Jack. I don't like the business anyhow.'

I retorted roundly, 'Which of us does? I'll tell you plain, if your man's content to fire in the air so will I. But I shall need an assurance.'

He rose from the table. 'I can't give it, Mr Sturrock. I'll convey that to Dashwood but neither can I say what he'll answer. And for now I'll leave you to make your dispositions.'

A very correct gentleman, I mused, watching him go, tossing a coin to the serving man, while Mr Digby himself watched me in turn from under his eyebrows. He said at last, 'If you're thinking to arrange it, Mr Sturrock, I wouldn't trust Dashwood that much. If you ask my advice you'll shoot first and shoot straight. But if you want me to stand as second I've no objection.'

'I'm persuaded it will all pass off to everybody's satisfaction,' I said. 'So we'll meet at Hyde Park Fields by Park Lane at nine. But for now...' I affected to hesitate, stroking my chin in doubt. 'There's a question or two if you'll bear with me, Mr Digby.'

For one instant the smoke stopped ascending from his pipe. 'What questions? And what's this about French spies at Drury Lane?'

'What?' I cried in pretended vexation. 'Has that got about?'

'It's all over the place. I never heard such poppycock.'

'I wish it was,' I answered, now affecting confusion. 'It's a serious business. Tell me now, have you ever heard of a certain Captain Pink? Otherwise known as the Gentleman's Provider.'

He gazed at me. 'I'll be damned if I have.'

This was hardly surprising as I had never heard of the

fellow myself until that moment, but it sounded well enough though somewhat like The Beggar's Opera; a work of which I much disapprove. 'He's a Free Trader,' I continued, 'a smuggler plying from Ipswich; brandy and tobacco and suchlike. But also letters and intelligences, and now and again a French agent in and out by way of the Low Countries.' I leaned across the table, full of mystery. 'Now here's the way of it, Mr Digby. We've reason to think he was in the theatre, back stage, the night Mr Mytton was killed.'

'D'you mean to say Bob Mytton didn't kill himself after all? He was murdered?'

I contrived to look vexed again. 'Nothing of the sort. We're satisfied on that score. But we don't know how deep that unhappy young gentleman was in with Captain Pink. What we're after is who saw the rogue, and what place and time. Somewhat of a dandy, though a weatherbeaten face. Blue coat with out steel buttons and usually affects a powdered wig for all he wears an eye patch.'

Mr Digby shook his head and I fancied he was laughing at me on the quiet; which suited my plans well enough. 'I didn't see the fellow; that's certain.'

'I wonder who did?' I mused. 'Where was you, Mr Digby, about the time of that fanfare of trumpets?'

He tapped the ash out of his pipe and took another light from the candle. 'Why on the stage wings watching that fantastical spectacle.'

'And Mr Dashwood and Lilley?'

'So was they.'

Still musing, the very picture of a poor Simple Simon, I asked, 'Yet you was all in the passage, by that door, when I arrived there myself.'

'That's easy enough if you came round from the pit, under the stage; we had but to go up the stairs. As I remember Dashwood went off a minute or so before and then Lilley and me followed him.'

I was at my most benevolent. 'So now we have it clear; and it's no great matter. But I had the notion somehow that you was all playing cards with Mr Cullen in the dressing room.'

'Then God knows where you got it from.'

'It's no matter,' I announced again, getting up. 'And I'm obliged to you, Mr Digby. Though it looks as if I shall have to go to Ipswich; see if I can pick up some trace there of this rascal, Captain Pink. I'd best take the next coach after we've got our business done in the morning.'

Mr Digby gave a short laugh. 'Then if you want to take it you'll do as I've told you. Fire quick and aim sure.'

'I'm obliged to you,' I repeated, settling my beaver and going out slowly to give Maggsy time to extricate himself and follow me.

He appeared out of the doorway like a minor demon in the murk and I drew him on a few yards for us to be swallowed in the fog before asking, 'Well?'

'Not a lot,' he announced. 'Cullen was asaying, "She sails with the tide first light on Monday," and t'other says, "Well, thank God it's of a Sunday anyhow, there'd be questions asked if I wasn't at the theatre," but then you come up and they stopped.'

'As you observe,' I said, 'it's not a lot. But as Mr Shakespeare also observed, " 'Tis not so deep as a well, nor so wide as a church door; but 'tis enough, 'twill serve." Let us go to our own fireside now; we've much to do tomorrow. Item for you, to make your way to either The City of Ramsgate, The Prospect of Whitby, or The Grapes Tavern at Wapping, there deliver a letter to my old friend Captain Bolton and bring back his answer.'

'You'll have my feet wore down to my knees,' the horrible little rogue grumbled. 'I wants to see the duel and there's no use of letters anyhow, you'll never be alive to have the answer; ain't you got it into your noddle yet that it's sticking out as plain as a whore's tits they mean to kill you?'

'You lewd monster,' I said, 'an all wise Providence is always and forever putting things into my head. And one of these at this instant is it's Mr Jack Dashwood they mean to kill, not me. So since I've already announced that I'll not shoot the fool what will they do next? You shall see the duel, Master Maggsy; perhaps to find out. And now come home, I say.'

CHAPTER EIGHT

It was a fit morning for pistol balls and sudden death, being unseasonable dank and misty, once more with the stink of sea coal and autumn in the air; and none of us spoke much as we rattled along Oxford Street, where there were few others save work people of the commoner sort abroad. For myself I was composing various philosophical reflections suitable to the occasion, such as the mutability of human affairs, whether the unseen Hand of Providence could stop a ball if it happened to be aimed straight, and which of the pistols I could contrive to get. I had little doubt of the outcome, being on the side of the Lord; but even He must turn to other matters or take a little cat nap from time to time. Dr Blossum also was somewhat speechless, part through carrying my armament and powder flask as if they was serpents which might turn and bite him, but more from having consumed the biggest breakfast I had ever seen any man pack away, much less a starving scribbler. Even Maggsy was uncommonly silent, but at last he announced, 'I don't doubt you'll split him but there's a good chance he'll split you as well and there goes my bread and butter and veal pies; however I'll take your letter to the old sea captain and tell him how you ended; one thing, you'll have the biggest funeral ever, half the villains in London'll turn out to see you put under and all cry, "God bless Hallelujah" for it.'

Having weightier matters to think about I paid little attention to the gloomy rogue, and by then coming to the top end of Park Lane close by where the old Tyburn

Gallows used to stand—demolished after the last hanging in '83, Newgate then being considered more pleasurable and convenient for all concerned—we set him off there to go about his own business. This being to quarter the belt of bushes and trees which lay down the side of the fields against the Lane, and to use his wits if he found any sign of emergencies or suspicious rascals lurking there, as I fancied there might be. Simple instructions; but I myself would sooner face the Prince of Darkness in person than Master Maggsy with the freedom of instructions like that and his own natural wickedness.

We ourselves turned left down the Lane as far as the reservoir entrance and bidding the hackney to wait in spite of the expense, for it is unseemly to stint on occasions like these, we set to walking under the elms with a few sad brown leaves floating down upon us through the mist; and again a good thick cover; better than enough to hide a dozen villains though, even if my notion was correct, I doubted there would be more than one. With no such worldly thoughts himself our Dr Blossum was moved to philosophise, observing on the closeness of the Deadly Reaper, but also on that damned book he could have done for me at a guinea a week; 'Your name inscribed upon it,' he said, ever hopeful, 'and a memorial long after mere flesh is dissolved away to dust.'

At length we were joined by Mr Digby, as bleak faced as ever and a little put out that we hadn't provided a hackney for him—which had slipped my memory—and at the same time a clatter of horses in the Lane heralded two more carriages. These discharged Dashwood and Lilley, a sober fellow that by the look of him was the surgeon, and Mr Cullen from one; and from the other, where they must have been packed like herrings in a barrel, a motley crew of blades and dandies making merry as if they were to attend a rare show or pyrotechnic display. I regarded this rout with some disfavour and when Messrs Cullen and

Lilley approached, looking solemn enough themselves, I observed plainly, 'You are late, gentlemen. Doubtless you waited to issue tickets for the performance.'

Standing a little aside himself Mr Dashwood very near choked on his rage and Cullen announced, 'By God, sir, that's uncivil. Can't we conduct this affair decent? Are your seconds present?'

'You'll never see 'em plainer,' I answered, presenting Mr Digby and the good doctor, who in his agitation took a great pinch of snuff and at once let out the most monstrous bellow of a sneeze, thus offending Dashwood yet more.

'What?' he cried. 'That damned scribbler? A mere starving windbag for a second? I'll not have it.'

So challenged the doctor himself looked like some fine round retort, and not all that philosophical, but Mr Cullen interposed. 'No, Jack, let it be. Mr Sturrock may choose who he likes.' He turned to Digby. 'A word with you, Mr Digby, if you please.'

They also drew apart and I watched them talking together, Mr Cullen shaking his head, while beside me Dr Blossum fizzled and rumbled deep in his belly, either from choler or that vast steak together with veal pie he had consumed. But then my man returned, with the hidden laugh which you could fancy but not quite see upon his face. Speaking very quiet he said, 'Dashwood refuses any accommodation.'

So it was to hang on the pistols; but I was no less confident of that. Though excellent pieces by Robert Wogdon of London they each have their own particular tricks, one firing high and the other a trifle to the left; this last never having been quite the same since I near enough brained a highwayman with it in a tavern on Hounslow Heath. I had but to observe which of the two Dashwood chose, act accordingly and trust in the Lord. 'Can't we have the business done?' I asked. 'I've other matters to attend to.'

They went about the farcical performance in due ceremony and order enough to make a cat laugh with its arse. Messrs Digby and Cullen measuring out the powder, tamping down the wads and balls with our Dr Blossum and the actor Lilley as observers, one still rumbling and simmering and the other white to the lips; Dashwood standing over by his supporters trying to raise an easy laugh, while I surveyed the cover of trees and bushes not twelve paces away. If Master Maggsy was there watching, as he should have been by now, there was no sign of him; nor was there any of the intruder he should be looking for. But there was time yet.

Then Mr Cullen enquired, 'Are we all satisfied, gentlemen? And are the two parties ready?' turning to present the pistols stocks outward, while Dashwood came over from his cronies to stand beside me. 'As the challenged person,' Cullen announced, 'Mr Sturrock has the right of choice.'

'It's of no matter,' I replied carelessly. 'They're both identical.' Nevertheless, knowing the look of them like my own hands, I was careful to pick the one which throws high. Dashwood must needs be damned lucky to hit me with the other unless he knew the left handed trick of it.

Having kept silent so far the surgeon spoke up now. 'Gentlemen, you've satisfied each other you're both willing. Why not say honour's satisfied and give up? You'll both be warned that if one is struck fatally the other may be charged with murder.'

'That be damned,' some rascal among the bystanders called out. 'What d'you think we've drove out here for? Remember the coffee pot, Jack. It's but a few days in Newgate and you'll be acquitted a hero.'

'Mr Dashwood,' I said sternly, 'take the surgeon's advice and retire. Another minute and it'll be too late. I can't warn you plainer.' As indeed I couldn't, for both Digby and Cullen were standing close and if, as I thought, they were in the plot I wanted to see it proved.

'I'll be damned if I will,' he answered between his teeth; the puppy had guts within him of a sort.

'Then you will stand back to back at my cane,' Cullen announced. 'When I count three you will take ten paces apiece and then turn, take aim, and wait until I cry "Fire".'

Seemingly there was no help for it, and we stood as he commanded with our pistols cocked and raised and then started to march the ten slow steps before we turned to face, looking at each other sideways to present the smallest target. I fancied I saw a movement in the bushes but could not be sure of it as I had other matters on my mind; for I will confess that not being in the heat of battle, when irritation gives a certain zest, it is a devilishly untoward experience to observe the muzzle of a pistol coming down at you and to see the black hole of it. With a prayer to my Maker, however, I reflected that I had only to lean to my own left when Cullen gave the signal and with the left handed throw of Dashwood's weapon his ball would fly past harmless enough.

But the ways of Providence are ever inscrutable and a most untoward circumstance arose. Either agitated by the solemn moment, or more likely from that monstrous steak lying on his belly, the fine flowery doctor chose this quiet hush to break wind in a most cavernous fart which echoed in the misty and breathless silence like a clap of thunder. It was very near the end of me. For in the roar of laughter, cries of 'Shame!' and my own discomposure, that damned unsportsmanlike young whelp Dashwood discharged at me before the order. Never have I known such a dastard's trick. I saw the flash, felt the ball fly past my ear by not more than a hairs breadth and, not unreasonably offended, fired back; but still to miss the rascal, though close enough to frighten him.

At that instant, hard on the bark of my own weapon, there came another lighter crack from the bushes and Dashwood jerked and dropped his arm, turned on me a look of pitiful astonishment and fell. I stayed no longer. With all the others rushing on him, sundry cries, exclamations, etc., Dr Blossum roaring, 'Choicely well done, sir,' there rose another screech which passed unheeded. It could only have come from Master Maggsy and, still carrying my own pistol, in six long strides I plunged into the covert myself.

Screened from the field there was an agitation and breaking ahead like a fearful struggle, and I crashed on myself somewhat concerned over Maggsy. But I need not have worried for there broke out again his own particular horrible curses coupled with others of a deeper key but no less lewd, and as I burst through the last bushes, close against Park Lane by now, I found him clinging to some other rogue or villain like a terrier to a bull; and being flung about much like one too. There was no time for niceties for our adventurous child was plainly getting the worst of it, but fortunately the fellow's hat had fallen off and I gave him one sharp quietus with my pistol which felled him like a log; and very likely put the barrel of that one out too, I reflected.

It was a rough looking lout dressed as the lower sort commonly are, frieze coat and britches, dirty cotton stockings, a skin weskit; and a fresh ragged scar across the side of his face from eye to ear. Clearly enough the sweet angel I'd put my mark on in that affray the other night; one, Tasker, also of Drury Lane. But he was lying quiet enough now, like to do so for some time by the look of him, and I said, 'So ho, Master Maggsy, we're doing very well, we're gathering the rogues together. But you left your action late, you little villain: I fear he's killed Mr Dashwood.'

'God's Truth,' Maggsy complained, 'can't I never get nothing right? Was of two minds what to do anyway. Only come upon him the last minute, he was that well hid and me having to move quiet; then I see he was ready with a pistol like you expected, and I says, "What ho, suppose he turns that on me?" which I don't fancy; so I reckons to let him blaze it off, when it won't be no more harm, but dig up a tussock of turf to fling and spoil his aim. I might've chucked it quick if he'd been sighting on you, but then I see he's after Mr Dashwood likewise as you said; I'll admire you're a good guesser. So I conclude there ain't much harm in that but still reckons to heave the turf as you say also you want Dashwood alive. Only all three of you went and banged off so damnation sudden it took me by surprise; it was a right mess then.'

'What happened?'

'Well he catched sight of me but I made to follow him and he chucked the pistol at me. Then I fell arse above tip over a tree root and the bastard come back like a fighting cock; lucky you was about, he'd ha' filleted me else. It's that cove Tasker from the Lane, ain't it? Have you killed him?'

'I doubt it,' I said. 'Like all of these rogues he'll have a good thick skull; it's his neck will give first. We must find that pistol, and quick about it.'

We set to hurriedly and a very short search discovered it; discovered something else too, for a pretty, elegant piece it was, not the sort of ironmongery you'd expect a low rogue of this kind to handle; mounted in silver after the Frenchy style and signed by Boutet of Versailles. In brief, a pair to the weapon which had killed Mr Robert Mytton.

Hard on this Dr Blossum came puffing and wheezing his way through the bushes, almighty pleased with himself and observing, 'It's an oddity of a way for a philosopher to pass his morning; but a diversion, no doubt of it, a rare diversion. I'm no judge of these matters, Mr Sturrock, but a monstrous fine shot that was, a clever piece of work.'

'What of Dashwood?' I demanded. 'Is he dead?'

'Dead?' Dr Blossum repeated. 'Why far from it. He's passing his time between cursing and swooning, putting on as fine a performance of heroics as you ever saw on the boards at Drury Lane. 'Twas but a flesh wound in the shoulder. And his fellows take it discourteous of you to march off the field so without stopping to see what damage you've done.' He stopped, gazing at our Sleeping Beauty upon the ground. 'Why what's this? Another one? You'll permit me to observe, Mr Sturrock, that you're a most uncommonly riotous man.'

'It's a riotous matter,' I answered, 'but we must go back; I still have business there.' Yet we had other business first, and I took Master Maggsy by the ear to rivet his attention, continuing, 'We've no time to bandy words so listen to your instructions now and take special note of 'em. You'll withdraw out of sight until this villain stirs; and when he does you'll follow and not let him out of your sight. I want to know who he reports to on the way, if any, and where he goes to ground so we can have him when we need him.'

The little monster nodded, his eyes alight with mischief, and I added further, 'You'll then go on to deliver the letter which I've given you to Captain Isaac Bolton. The three taverns in Wapping where he's most likely to be found are written there, and you may take all day if that's how it goes but without fail I must have his answer back by tonight. Time's at our heels now.' In my urgency and not wishing any failure for lack of disbursement I actually thrust a handful of coins at him, several shillings and perhaps even a florin or two; an extravagance which I reflected on soberly afterwards, suspecting the wretch had kept some part of that largesse for himself. But this was no occasion for counting the pennies, and saying, 'Now set about it, and don't fail me or I'll have the hide off your back,' I finished, 'So come Dr Blossum; we'll go and pay our respects.'

We were very near too late, for with his shoulder bandaged and his fellows still making an extravaganza of it, they were supporting Dashwood to the carriage, pale but proud. As the custom is with these affairs the fallen is not permitted to curse, revile or otherwise abuse the victor, but Mr Dashwood was plainly offended. Nevertheless I said, 'Well, sir, I'm thankful the matter's no worse and I hope you now feel that honour's satisfied.' He did not answer and I continued, 'For myself I'll announce to all in hearing that you're a brave man; and if I once made some ill considered remark concerning coffee pots I'll withdraw the imputation.'

By all except Dashwood that was considered to be a particular genteel remark, and there was some applause for it before they started to climb into the carriages; Mr Digby casting a sideways look at Dr Blossum and electing to ride with Cullen, which also suited me. Then before the surgeon could mount I drew him aside. 'What of the wound?' I enquired.

'A mere nothing,' he replied. 'He's the luckiest fellow alive; so are you for that matter. A few inches more to the right and you'd have done for him.'

It was clear that even this fellow imagined I had fired the shot, but I let it pass. I asked, 'Have you removed the ball yet?'

'I shall do so at his lodging.'

'Then, sir,' I said, 'I most importantly charge and require you to preserve that ball and to send it to me this day at my chambers above Mrs Spilsbury's Dispensary in Soho Square. The ball and a statement signed by yourself certifying you extracted it, together with the address of Mr Dashwood's lodging.'

'Begod,' he observed, for these surgeons are always full of importance, 'you give your orders.'

'I do sir,' I agreed, 'and with the power of the law behind 'em. More I cannot say, but there's matter in this business touching the peace and good order of our Lord, the King, and his subjects.'

It was a fine ringing phrase, but he gave me a damned odd look and answered shortly, 'Very well then, if you make such a bother of the thing; I'll send it by my apprentice. But I must look to my patient now.'

So I was left the victor on the field with Dr Blossum, who was priming himself up with snuff in evident satisfaction. 'A rare diverting morning's entertainment,' he pronounced. 'Choicely good and a happy outcome. I'd have grieved to see a man who's of a mind to patronise a book laid low. There ain't so many of 'em about. But now you're at ease should we not retire to some tavern or coffee house and there consider a contract?'

That is ever the way of these starveling scribblers, they take you at your lightest word; if you give them a breakfast they'll expect a dinner, give them a dinner and the next time they'll look for a banquet. But I had a kindness for the poor, simple soul and I replied, 'That's something which demands long consideration, Dr Blossum, and so far from being set at ease I've grave affairs to settle and must make haste about it. At present I'll take you back as far as Soho Square in my hackney and we'll engage to meet for further discussion when we've more time for it.' With that he had to be content though I had a certain sympathy for the man but not to the extent of a guinea a week. However kindly inclined you should never give these scribblers a word of encouragement.

For myself I went on to Bow Street where I reported to my master to show that I understand my place. Happily there was a heavy court that day and he had little time to spare; also being a trifle testy with the gout, and half persuaded that the whole Drury Lane affair was a mere fancy of my own, he was of two minds about calling me off it altogether. This seemed to be a fortunate omen to produce Mr Mytton the elder's letter, which I had obtained for some such emergency as this and perhaps others, as I then did. There was of course certain observations on my manners, impudence, general irregularities and sundry other matters, but in the end the good gentleman calmed suddenly and demanded, 'Well, what are you waiting for, man? Get out of my sight and about the business then.'

Thus I contrived to place the investigation on a more secure and regular footing without disclosing much of what I was now very sure lay beyond it, namely the robbery or purloinage of a shipment of gold this coming Sunday. It was a happy conclusion, for there was little doubt that any such disclosure would have set Mr A. sending hot foot with a warning for Mr Mytton the elder to the great detriment of my own stratagems. I had no great love of Mr Mytton, and I had also to consider my own just rewards and profits while yet seeing justice done.

Duty and respect being so discharged and the day turning out finer than it had first threatened, also being of no mood to incur any further expenses in the way of hackneys, I walked comfortably as far as the famous Grecian Coffee House in Devereux Court off Fleet Street—another resort which the genteel visitor to London should not miss as here you may sometimes have the most profound discussions on matters of the day—and then on by easy stages to the Cornhill. I discovered the Cornhill Coffee House close by the Royal Exchange, and if the Grecian is a haunt where you will hear learned and literary discourse this other was a very hive of the bees and ants about their mysterious affairs.

I surveyed the gentlemen of this busy scene through the haze of tobacco smoke, all of a certain sharpness and most not without a kind of resemblance to Mr Mytton himself. Beaver hats and sober clothes, some of them frowning over the day's newsprints, others making notes in little books, but more still conferring in groups with various cabalistic utterances and wiseacre faces; even the aproned waiters hurrying from one party to another and so far as I could observe passing more messages than serving refreshment. But there was no sign of Mr Grabble even though the hour was now approaching half after one.

With some irritation I moved about the tables and high backed seats searching for him and at last one of the waiters, as if jealous of a stranger here, stayed long enough to enquire, 'Are you looking for some gentleman, sir?'

'Mr Grabble,' I said, 'of Mytton and Company.'

The fellow's face changed at that. He repeated, 'Mr Grabble, sir; oh dear, that's vexatious,' and broke off to cry, 'Coming, gentlemen! I can't be all places at once. Mr Grabble,' he continued again to me, 'there's a shocking thing now; haven't you heard? It's all over the City.'

'Dammit,' I answered, 'what is?'

'A moment, sir,' he replied, 'a moment only,' and this time called out, 'Mr Tullet, sir; message for Mr Tullet there. Mr Jenkin said you was to be sure and wait for him; the big Mr Jenkin.'

'Come now,' I demanded, 'when you can spare me half an instant, what's this about Grabble?' But already I was fearing the worst, and not all that surprised.

'The Fleet Ditch,' that damnation waiter started and then broke off yet again to touch another pursey little fellow on the arm and whisper at him, 'Word from you-know-who, sir; says to tell you particular. Pearl Reefs won't hold up above tomorrow forenoon.'

'Then keep it quiet,' the other hissed, sparing a moment to give me a malevolent look before he darted away.

Fast losing patience I said, 'Will you come to it, man. What's happened to Grabble?'

'Why, are you a bit thick?' he asked. 'Ain't I telling you? Found in the Fleet Ditch by watchmen this morning.'

Even then he could not finish for yet another pushed up, thrusting me aside uncivilly to beg, 'What's this, Barker; what's this I hear? Is it true the *Esmeralda* brig's foundered off the Manacle Rocks?'

'Not as I know of, sir,' he rejoined. 'Nor they ain't heard of it at Lloyd's; that I'm sure of. Where did you have it from?'

'Post boy,' that one wailed, vanishing into the crowd like a wraith. 'Post boy riding hard from Cornwall.'

'Damnation,' I announced between my teeth, 'I'll have this out of you, my man, if I have to drag you into the street to get it.'

'God's sake,' he protested, 'I'm telling you; if you'd only listen. He was found in the Fleet Ditch this morning either bludgeoned or stabbed to death; some say one thing, some t'other. It's a most vexatious occurrence.'

'Indeed it is,' I agreed. 'Vexatious for me coming all the way from Soho to see him; and particular vexatious for Mr Grabble. How do they know it was him?'

'Found letters on the poor gentleman so addressed. Coming, sir,' the fellow cried again, 'coming, I say,' and vanished into the press like a minnow leaving me to retire to the comparative quietness of the Cornhill street with this disturbing intelligence. There was little doubt that this business was taking a very ugly turn.

CHAPTER NINE

The hour now advancing I repaired to an adjacent eating house which looked commodious—these of the City being famous, for our bankers must needs keep up their strength —and dined moderately on three dozen oysters, a very fair saddle of mutton, and a Stilton; the quality middling good but the price extortionate. Apart from that however I was not displeased; and while I was about this comfortable repast it gave me leisure to reflect on the sad end of Mr Grabble, the present unfolding of this singular plot and mystery, and what stratagems I myself should set about next.

Several matters were abundantly clear. Item, that having set the whole game afoot by his foolish tongue these several weeks ago, Mr Grabble had finally wagged that unruly member once too often and most likely no later than last night. Another, that Mr Jack Dashwood was in some danger also, and such danger must of necessity arise from certain knowledge he had, something he had seen or heard, whether he realised it himself or not. And one more, that these damnable villains were moving with remorseless speed and ruthlessness, and if I wanted to lay 'em all by the heels I must go just as fast and sure myself. There was no virtue in taking the two ringleaders if all the other rogues were to scatter and vanish. We must have them in the very act of their knavery; the more so as that was the only way I could see to my own profit and reward. Even in the Art and Science of Detection the labourer is worthy of his hire.

On these reflections I ventured the expense of yet another hackney back to Soho Square. Maggsy had not yet returned but there was a packet from the excellent surgeon who, as good as his word, enclosed the ball he had extracted from Mr Dashwood and a brief note; this giving Dashwood's lodging, also in Bloomsbury Market very close by Mrs. Huxey's house, and stating that apart from fever or mortification the patient could be expected to make a fair recovery, the ball having lodged in the flesh without striking bone anywhere. That was a fortunate circumstance, as I had questions to put to Mr Dashwood next; and taking the ball, one of my own weapons, and that fanciful little French pistol—which you must not imagine I had left lying in the bushes at Hyde Park Fields—I set out on my travels once more.

I was admitted to the house by a severe female dressed in black bombazine and a very look of lodging keeper about her. With a certain pomp, as if she at once feared the worst and yet looked to take pleasure from it, she led me up the stairs and announced in a hushed voice, 'Lady Dorothea Hookham and Mrs Huxey are with him,' so admitting me also to the chamber. True enough our wounded hero was sitting propped up in his bed, a look of poetic suffering and left arm in a black sling, with Mrs Huxey ministering at one side and Lady Dorothea from the other. It was a genteel and elevating sight and I felt almost constrained to shed a tear or two myself. Mrs Huxey gazed at me stormily, her bosoms swelling like the waves unsubdued, and Lady Dorothea said, 'We did not look to see you, Mr Sturrock. Have you not done enough for one day?'

Thinking that by the way it looked here she would get her husband and Mr Dashwood his coalfields I did my best French bow, but answered, 'No, ma'am, I have not. I have not done near enough.'

'If you wish to enquire of Mr Dashwood's health,' she said, 'you may do so. And I shall then ask you to leave.'

I bowed to her again. 'With all respect, ma'am, you'd

find it difficult; we've a small slight matter of attempted murder to investigate.'

Mrs Huxey let out a scream; she couldn't have bettered it on Drury Lane. 'La, what fearful things the monster talks of. I declare I shall swoon.'

'Must you go on like this?' Dashwood demanded pettishly. 'My head aches and this shoulder you presented me with throbs most damnably. Dorothea, my angel, I could take another sip of chamomile.'

'And you're lucky to take even that,' I rejoined. 'The shoulder you speak of was not presented by me, but by some villain concealed in the trees who fired to kill you. And I mean to know why.'

Upon that Mrs Huxey did swoon, flopping back in a chair but keeping one eye open with a lively curiosity while Lady Dorothea asked sharply, 'What is this, Mr Sturrock?'

'Why, God's Blood,' Dashwood cried, 'a cursed, blasted lie. He was out to do for me; that's plain, and be damned to him.'

Mrs Huxey let out a moan at that but Lady Dorothea observed, 'Mr Dashwood, we may dismiss your language for this present as you are not well, but when you are about again I think we must amend it a little.' But she looked at me sharper than ever and asked again, 'What is this? Have you proof of it?'

Thinking that Mr Dashwood might not have his coalfields so cheap after all, I declared, 'All the proof in the world, ma'am' and produced the two pistols and the ball. I continued, 'Item; the pistol which I fired this morning. Item; the pistol which was discovered when I observed some rogue making his escape through the bushes into Park Lane. Item; the ball extracted from Mr Dashwood's shoulder and testified to by the surgeon.'

Mrs Huxey let out a fine screech, but Lady Dorothea silenced her and looked to me to go on. I was coming to think better of her every minute despite her Whiggish notions and said, 'Now observe. We place the ball in my own pistol.' This I did showing that although pretty close as to size it dropped in loose and even rattled in the barrel. 'If you fired that it wouldn't carry true for five paces, much less twenty. So observe again.' I rolled it out of the barrel and slipped it into the French pistol where it settled true and snug. 'You're lucky it was near enough spent when it struck you, Mr Dashwood,' I concluded. 'And I'm fortunate that it's not flattened out of shape.'

Lady Dorothea looked from Mr Dashwood to me. 'I don't pretend to understand these things; but this seems plain.' She got a touch of the high and mighties. 'Why did you allow the man to escape?'

'There was no choice about it,' I answered. 'He'd got too good a start and I was more concerned with Mr Dashwood himself at that instant. But don't fret, ma'am, here's the important matter; that'll hang him in the end and several others with him.' I tossed the French pistol down on the bed causing another screech from Mrs Huxey, and asked, 'Let's have it clear, Mr Dashwood. Have you ever seen that before? Or one precisely like it?'

White to the lips the fellow answered, 'I never have. Hell's damnation, what's all this leading up to?'

With Lady Dorothea listening intently, Mrs Huxey uttering little cries, I explained the whole circumstance and finished, 'In short a plot to silence you, Mr Dashwood, and put me out of the way. For had that shot killed you I'd have been in Newgate in a matter of hours; and no examining the size of the ball and the bore of my pistol either. It takes a man of my stamp to think of things like that. A clever plot in its way, making quick use of a situation; the same cleverness we've seen at Drury Lane of late. A plot set up by somebody as knew my expressed intention of firing at you to miss.'

Mrs Huxey let out another wail at that. 'Are you

proposing I had some hand in it, sir?'

'I am not, ma'am,' I assured her. 'For I know that of all people you're the least like to do Mr Dashwood a mischief.' I looked hard at him and he took my message; namely that I was apprised of his relation with that good generous woman. He too glanced sideways at Lady Dorothea and back at me, and I said, 'I'd be infinitely obliged if the ladies would leave us to have a word or two alone, Mr Dashwood.'

For an instant it looked as if Lady Dorothea would climb on her high horse again, but Dashwood could take a hint as well as the next man; he perceived which side his muffin was buttered on and cried, 'Let it be, Dorothea, my angel. We'd best humour the fellow and get it over sooner.'

'And very wise,' I agreed waiting for the door to close behind the ladies, though they went somewhat reluctantly. 'There're things you wouldn't like Lady Dorothea to hear about, Mr Dashwood, and I see no need to tell her so long as you keep me in a good humour. An exercise which you don't show much aptitude for so far.'

'Tell her what?' he demanded through his teeth, looking very near as wicked as he had this morning when he aimed that pistol so damned close to my ear.

'For one,' I said, 'the nature of your negotiations with Isaacs and Fettelson through Mr Tom Cullen.'

Had it been possible he'd have turned paler still, but he managed to whisper, 'What of God's Name is this?'

'Don't you know?' I enquired kindly. 'Well then, Isaacs and Fettelson do business in the way of expectations. That is they'll advance money on what young gentlemen might be expected to inherit or otherwise pick up not too far ahead. In your case it's that part of the Hookham estates and the coalfields with 'em that come to Lady Dorothea and as good as come to you when the marriage settlement's signed.' I shook my head at him. 'She wouldn't like it, Mr Dashwood. There's no doubt the lady wants a husband, she wants to get an heir to please her poor old father as soon as may be, and she'll take you if she must; but she wouldn't stomach that.'

The fellow was ashen, yet still with spirit of a sort. 'God damn your eyes,' he retorted. 'What d'you want? Money? You're a common thieftaker. It's all you fellows are ever after.'

'Don't try my patience too far, Mr Dashwood,' I advised him in the soft and terrible voice which quells even Maggsy. 'I want the truth of all you saw and heard in the theatre that night Mr Mytton was killed.'

He looked at me sidelong. 'I always thought there was something fishy about that.'

'As fishy as a herring barrel,' I agreed. 'And you more than thought so; you were sure of it. Now then; the fatal moment was that fanfare of trumpets and cannon on the stage. I know all the answers or I can guess 'em, but I want to have it proved so don't try no lies. According to Mr Tom Cullen you were all playing cards in the gentlemen's general dressing room; himself and you, Mr Digby and Lilley.'

He gazed at me, his mouth agape. 'No such thing. Digby, Lilley and me were watching that spectacle from the wings.'

'Yet when Mr Cullen told me you were playing whist Lilley was present and did not deny it.'

Dashwood essayed a laugh. 'Lilley owes him money. In such a case you don't deny Tom Cullen. For all his Gentleman Jim ways he's a regular roaring boy.'

'I'm coming about to think so myself. Now then, as I understand it you left the stage first and Digby and Lilley followed a minute or so after. You went up to the dressing room passage?' He nodded, and I asked, 'What did you observe there?'

'Be damned...' he started, but then muttered, 'Why Tom Cullen and Boosey; by the ladies' door whispering together. Boosey said, "Wisht now, it's Mr Dashwood," and Cullen looked round over his shoulder and cried out,

"God's Teeth, Jack, there's something amiss here." '

'And which of 'em was thrusting some object, as it might have been a key, into his pocket?'

The poor rogue did not want to answer that; for a minute indeed I was afraid that he might truly fall into a fever, but I pressed him and at last he admitted, 'Tom Cullen.'

'We're doing very nicely,' I encouraged him, 'but what else is there, Mr Dashwood? Which of 'em was it mentioned that if you discovered any fanciful notions, or spoke out of turn, Lady Dorothea might come to hear of your dealings with Isaacs and Fettelson?' That was a mere shot at venture but by the look of his face it went home and, quick to take my advantage, I admonished him, 'Out with it, Mr Dashwood, or I might think of telling the lady myself.'

'Digby,' he confessed unwillingly. 'But not so much like that. That horrible little creature of yours brought it about, nosing around by then and roaring, "God's Tripes, I'm going to fetch old Sturrock," and Cullen asked, "Who the devil's Sturrock?" '

'What?' I demanded, mortally offended. 'D'you mean to say he didn't know?'

'Seemingly not. Boosey answered, "He's a Bow Street man; and a right damnation, wind and piss, strutting inquisitive turkey cock." '

There was a certain note of malice on this astonishing pronouncement and I mused, 'So ho. I shall reflect on that observation when I watch Mr Boosey hang; and others with him. Pray continue, Mr Dashwood.'

'Digby said, "Inquisitive, is he? Then it'd be a sad shame if he got to hear of Jack's dealings with Fettelson's over Lady Dorothea's fortune." '

'So you concluded to keep your mouth shut; and thus became an accessory. It appears to me,' I added severely, 'that you're all a sorry parcel of rogues, Mr Cullen in particular. How does he work for Isaacs and Fettelson? Is it like Mr Grabble with Mytton and Company? And what's his own situation as to fortune?'

'Not to say works for them. He's a kind of agent and takes his commission. As to fortune, I'd say it's devilish tight, for he lives like a fighting cock.'

'But he looks to mend it soon,' I observed, 'and so does Mr Digby. Well it's of some slight interest, but nothing I don't already know. Mr Grabble now; when did he first start chattering about this shipment of gold?'

The fellow's romantic curls were somewhat damp on his forehead, but he answered, 'Five, six weeks since.'

'And what's it worth? Did the little clatterjaw ever say that much?'

'There's a rumour of forty thousand pounds or more.'

'And a nice round sum.' A very tidy sum, I reflected, and if I could not get some small portion of it for my own due and just reward I should be a simpleton myself. 'Well worth a thought of planning and a few murders.'

'A few murders?' he asked, turning more ashen still.

'I make it four known to this instant. And very likely one more to come. Yours, Mr Dashwood,' I added benevolently.

Speechless at that he looked close enough to expiring on the pillows, and I said, 'Let me rehearse them. A kitchen girl to start with from Mr Robert Mytton's household. They might not have thought to kill her, poor soul, but they did; to the end of putting another pretty creature in her place. One known as Antimony Nell, whose part it is to poison or otherwise discommode Mr Mytton's footman-guard, so Master Boosey may take his place upon the coach and at some critical moment dispose of the coachman.'

I was becoming a little anxious about Mr Dashwood's health but went on, 'Mr Robert Mytton next because he'd rumbled the plot from one hint here and another there and was out to stop it. We may never know the details and they don't matter much now, but Messrs Cullen and Digby acted fast and certain. After that Mother Knapp, as she was guessing things herself, asking questions and opening her mouth too wide when drunk. And the latest, Mr Grabble.'

'Mr Grabble?' he repeated on a dying note.

'Found in the Fleet Ditch today,' I assured him. 'Shall we make a guess? Because he'd put two and two together also. He was threatening our villains to blow the business and stop the shipment altogether unless they paid him a share. They're a fearful lot, Mr Dashwood. I wonder why they're after you?'

'How do I know?' he cried. 'God's sake let me be.'

'Then again I must tell you myself. Because you tried the same game as Mr Grabble. In short, you'd keep your mouth shut at a price. And when did you make that offer?' He fell into another pale silence, and I said, 'Come now, Mr Dashwood, don't irritate me more.'

'The day after Bob Mytton was killed,' he confessed.

'Before or after the business of the coffee pot and that farcical duel proposed?'

'Before.'

'Who put you up to this duel?'

'Nick Lilley.'

'And Lilley's in debt to Cullen. God help you,' I observed in some wonderment, 'you'll never make a villain, you're too big a fool. When you marry Lady Dorothea you'd best go into Parliament. That's a sure and certain home for would-be rogues who ain't smart enough for felony. When and where is that coach to be attacked?'

He shook his head. 'I don't know.'

'Mr Dashwood,' I urged him, 'think of Lady Dorothea; and your own neck. When and where? Some time on Sunday; but when?'

'I tell you I don't know,' he near enough wept. 'I couldn't get it out of 'em.'

There was a ring of truth about that, however inconvenient, and taking the pistols to carry them away I rose with a last word. 'It's of no great matter, yet I'd like to know how Mr Robert Mytton got to hear of this plot.'

Thinking himself on somewhat more solid ground the fellow was all eagerness. 'What he picked up, I fancy. Ginny Posset told me two or three weeks back that Boosey had asked to be put up as footman in the Mytton household and Bob told him they was well satisfied with the men they had. Then again Bob observed to me that if Mr Mytton knew how much Mr Grabble was talking about his money matters he'd have a seizure; but he was damned if he was going to tell the old man as they were at loggerheads just then.'

'Was there anything near to the fatal night?'

'It might have been something Bob heard from Ginny this time. The night before. He happened on me in Ned's Coffee House latish on and asked had I heard anything of Digby coming into a legacy to which I answered that he was more like to come into a miracle. This he agreed, but then stopped and demanded, "Or is he, by God? By God, I wonder?" He stopped once more and finished, "Dashwood, do me a service, will you? Tell Digby I want to talk to him; tell him it's about legacies. Tomorrow after the performance; I'm out riding all day."'

'And did you?'

'I saw no harm in it. I thought it was part of the foolery with him and Digby and Ginny Posset. I told him at rehearsal in the forenoon.'

'Thus giving Digby time to confer with Cullen and Boosey and make their plans. It's a pretty business,' I mused. 'I wish I could see one single spark of human kindness in it anywhere; apart from your two ladies. And both of them better than you deserve.' I concluded, 'Now, Mr Dashwood, here are your instructions and you'll fail 'em at your peril. You will lie close here. It shall be put about that you're at death's door—as indeed you are—and on strict orders of the surgeon and Lady Dorothea nobody is to be admitted until better news is heard.'

Cutting short his objections with further pertinent obser-vations on his character, manners and future if I had my way, I called in the ladies again to close the debate; Mrs Huxey, the generous creature, continuing stormy and the bosoms yet like billows unsubdued, and Lady Dorothea still with a whiff of the mighties. A lesser man might have been daunted but after yet more compliments and instruc-tions like a surgeon, repeating most particular that they must keep Mr Dashwood close and turn away all callers, I bowed my respects to Mrs Huxey and begged the favour of a further word with my lady.

She preceded me out to the landing once more, dismissed the lodging keeper with a look which spoke volumes for equality, and enquired, 'What is this, Mr Sturrock? Mr Dashwood was feverish flushed; and you, I believe, are about some subterfuge.'

'Subterfuge, ma'am?' I asked, scandalised to my soul. 'What makes you fancy that? I wouldn't think of such a thing; I hope I know my place better. No, ma'am,' I con-tinued earnestly, 'we have here as ugly a business as ever I've seen, and I need help.'

'What ugly business?' she asked; she was shrewd enough, however crackpot otherwise.

'No less than a gang of monstrous desperados and mohocks about some uncommon wickedness this coming Sunday. So much I've picked up from certain hints and investigations this last few days, but the worst of it is I don't know precisely what they're up to, nor where.' There was no virtue in advising her they were out to rob Mr Mytton's coach of forty thousand pounds in gold, for the good lady would merely have me warn that tight-fisted banker or do so herself; to the detriment of my own small reward. Even in upholding the law a man must look to his own good.

I continued, 'The younger Mr Mytton was killed on

account of discovering some part of it and, as we've seen today, they had a try with Mr Dashwood for the same reason. The brave gentleman's volunteered what he knows, and it's of assistance, though little enough. And as to that, ma'am, I'd advise not to tax him with it, for it lies on his mind and you might fret him into a fever.'

She presented me a singularly thoughtful look. 'You are uncommonly solicitous, Mr Sturrock. Do you know who these villains are?'

'Some two or three; and I could take 'em up tonight. But that'd leave as many more at large, and I'll be plain with you, ma'am, they'd conclude that Mr Dashwood had passed the word. His life wouldn't be worth a tallow dip.' I added, 'To my knowledge they've killed four poor innocent souls already.'

That took her fair in the rigging. 'Dear God,' she whispered, 'what a dreadful place this is. Shall we ever see a just, equal, and innocent society, Mr Sturrock?'

Restraining my natural observations on that I answered, 'In Heaven perhaps, ma'am, but it's unlikely in London.'

She mused on this for a time and at last enquired, 'What help do you need?'

'To hasten my investigations tomorrow a light carriage or chaise and driver. And on Sunday as many good stout fellows and horses as you can muster from your establishment.'

By now the look became strangely quizzical. 'Are you proposing a battle then?'

'Indeed I hope not,' I protested. 'But unless I'm much mistaken this affair is something bigger and more audacious than has ever been attempted before.'

'And you've a great desire to set about it in your own way?' she asked, yet more quizzing. 'Don't we have officers of the law for these things?'

'Parish constables and watchmen? They'd run screaming. Or I could call for our whole Bow Street force; but we're all too few and already woefully overstretched. Again I might prevail upon my magistrate to apply for a company of militia, as can be done in extreme cases. Though with all the orders and instructions and approvals it would turn your hair white waiting for 'em. Speed and secrecy are of the essentials now, ma'am; and it's all quite regular. A Bow Street man or even a mere constable may call upon any citizen to assist him in preserving the King's peace.'

'So I understand. Tell me, how far is Mr Dashwood concerned?'

'Like so many of us, ma'am,' I announced carefully, 'Mr Dashwood is not always careful in his choice of friends. And like any spirited young gentleman he'll allow his loyalty to outrun his wisdom. But apart from that he's had no hand in it. If we arrange this matter as I hope to Mr Dashwood need never appear in it again.'

'I see.' She mused over me somewhat curiously again and at last said, 'Very well, Mr Sturrock. You shall have your carriage and horses and men. There are enough of them at Hanover Square; I sometimes wonder what they all find to do.'

'Ma'am,' I assured her, 'I'm infinitely obliged. And I'll engage that we shall settle this business to the whole end of Law and Justice and the best satisfaction of all concerned.'

So after some further arrangement that the carriage was to await orders outside my lodging in the early forenoon tomorrow, and with renewed protestations of gratitude and obedient humble respects from myself, we parted the best of friends. As I stood now if there was any reward to come I should have the handling of it alone, without any ungenteel discussion about how it was to be disposed of. But for the person of Lady Dorothea, I thought, sooner Mr Jack Dashwood than me; when she did get that bold fellow she'd have his flying feathers clipped in a week and make him a sober country gentleman in a month.

CHAPTER TEN

Not dissatisfied, though having gleaned little which I had
not already discovered by my own wit, I turned my steps
again to Soho Square through the bustle of Bloomsbury
Market. A phantasmagorick spectacle with the night and
mist descending, flaring torches casting an uncertain light,
your oranges and apples shining between shadowy figures,
urchins about their never ending devilment slipping and
skittering through the throng, and all assailed by the cries
of costermongers among their whelks, shrimps, jellied eels
and other vulgar delicacies. A scene such as I love to dwell
on when at leisure, but having more pressing business now.

I had but two problems remaining. One being where Mr
Mytton's coach, very certainly with Boosey on it, would be
bound for this Sunday; and the other, at what time of day.
The first, since our gold must be destined for the West
Indies, we knew would be a ship sailing on the morning
tide of Monday; this was the subject of my enquiry to the
excellent Captain Isaac Bolton, and I had particular hopes
for it. There is little that Isaac cannot tell you about London River from Adelphi Wharf to Rotherhithe.

The second, however, at what time the coach was expected and where the rogues meant to attack it would
admit of a wider solution. I will confess I was in some
perplexion here, as plainly with my own designs in mind I
could not go to Mr Robert Mytton hat in hand and ask
him in so many words; that forty thousand pounds would
never leave his strong room if I did. In that respect Mr
Grabble's death was doubly untimely for there was little
doubt that he had known. But I had yet a day to discover
it; that and the benevolence of the Lord Who, as we are
taught, prefers a poor man above a banker.

I reached my lodging to find Master Maggsy returned at last sitting with his boots off and toasting his feet at the fire, a most unlovely sight, while complaining loudly about the countless miles he had trudged, weariness, hunger, thirst and other sufferings. But there was a letter lying on the table and, ignoring the little imp's observations, I took it across to the candles. This is what it said in my good old friend's somewhat strange and lightning struck calligraphy.

'Jrmy; yr enquiries to hnd this inst. To the best of my infmtion. I hear of the *Nancy Drew*, 500 tons, sailing for the Indies from Greenland Dock by the tide of Monday; this being about the first light. An uncommon fast and handy ship; Captain Jos. Hardcastle; by nature like to name. Also carries armament above the ordinary and lately took aboard one Thos. Williams, a Welshman but reputed a master gunner. Also uncommon for a ship bound to the Indies to sail from Greenland, but may be that her slipping away from there will be less noted. Greenland D. is off Deptford Marshes up river of the Victualling Office and Dudman's Yard. As to yr knd enquiries of mslf. I do well enough for a paid off hulk. I come aboard little by little as the Master's Mate cried out seeing a one legged man at the capstan. Yr obnt friend, Isaac Bolton (Captn Retrd).'

'So ho,' I mused. 'Deptford Marshes, is it? A Godforsaken and desolate place, Master Maggsy; inhabited only by wildfowl and no doubt a few country savages lurking in the rushes. As our good sea captain says, we do indeed come aboard little by little.'

'You watch you don't go overboard all in one,' Maggsy said. 'They're a rare, low down guts ripping lot, these are. I'd as soon we went after a jolly highwayman with guineas ajingling in his pocket. Anyway I done very well. I reckon I'm doing it all for you.'

'All except the head work,' I reminded the impudent

rascal. 'And that's the greater part of the Art and Science of Detection. Now then, come to the rogue Tasker, this morning.'

'God's Truth,' he announced with relish, 'you must've give him a bouncer, I thought he was never going to come round, and then he sits there moaning and nursing his head and cussing; you never heard such language, things as even Mr William Makepeace'd never have thought of. In the end he crawls out and makes off across Park Lane into Wood's Mews.'

I shall spare you Maggsy's coarse account of our man's peregrinations but in the end he reached Blenheim Mews, off Oxford Street, and there went to ground in an ordinary; which is a common ale house frequented by grooms, ostlers, stable boys and others of the lower sort. Here he found himself a place at a settle while Maggsy with some resource edged himself into the other side of it, only separated from Tasker by the thickness of the boards between them; these high backed seats in most of our taverns, coffee and eating houses are a notable convenience in the Art and Science of Detection.

'And thankful enough to take the weight off my own feet,' Maggsy continued. 'So there we was and me watching him unknown; and after a time somebody else come in and sat down by him.'

'Not Cullen or Digby,' I said, 'they wouldn't appear in the open. So it was Boosey.'

'God's Whiskers,' Maggsy answered in disgust, 'there ain't no telling you nothing. It was Boosey right enough and he asks, "Well, Jake, how did you come off?" to which the other replies, "I done the job; a neat, pretty shot," and then Boosey leans across the table like he's about to throttle Master Jake and announces, "Well you're a damnation liar because I've just had word that come less than five minutes our man was sitting up as bright as a cockerel. Was you seen?"'

'What did he answer to that?' I asked.

'Never a word. I reckon this Master Tasker don't want to let on how he got knocked cold. He says, "The ball must've been near spent; I couldn't get no closer to him," and Boosey turns like old Holy Bones is sometimes, all sad and sorrowful, and replies, "You've failed me, Jake; I told 'em you was the dandy boy for this business and you've failed me. But let it be. Dashwood might yet die of an inflammation, though if he blabs to old Mytton by way of Lady Horse Piss our gentlemen won't thank you for it, Jake."'

I exclaimed at the low and vulgar manner these rascals refer to our nobility but said, 'Shall I tell you something, Master Maggsy? A strange and mysterious notion I have growing on me?'

'You get so many strange and mysterious notions,' the rude little villain retorted, 'that nothing'd surprise me. What's this one?'

'I shall not particularise,' I told him. 'Save to observe that like the ways of Providence those of bankers are dark and inscrutable. But I'll add this. It won't make a lot of difference if Mr Dashwood does blab. Continue with your tale. No doubt there was some argument about the pistol, as our man would not confess to leaving it in Hyde Park Fields?'

'That's right,' Maggsy agreed. 'You know it all, don't you? Tasker claims he's sticking to the pistol, being worth a few guineas to a poor man, and if the gentlemen don't like it they can kiss his arse; and anyway he ain't got paid out for Polly Knapp and Mr Grabble yet.'

'Polly Knapp and Mr Grabble,' I mused. 'So we've got our man for them, though it's no great matter. What else was there? There's nothing new in all of this. The one thing I want, boy, is time and place.'

'I'm coming to it.' The aggravating rogue was determined to tell the tale in his own way and continued, 'Well then Boosey says Mother Knapp and Mr Grabble is only worth a guinea apiece at the best and there shouldn't properly be nothing for Mr Dashwood, the job not being finished, likewise Tasker didn't do you as he should the other night, and he ain't found Holy Bones neither; all the same and not withstanding he'll still pick up his hundred guineas when the gentlemen come to pay out.'

'A very fair price,' I observed, 'for a very fair villain. We'll watch this one take the jump at Newgate, Master Maggsy; that I promise you.'

'Ain't much of a treat,' he replied. 'I don't reckon a lot on hangings, there's nothing to it; though I see a highwayman once as took twenty minutes to go, the crowd was counting in the end and the ladies swooning and screeching and chucking bunches of flowers at him.'

'Maggsy,' I asked, 'will you come back to Boosey while you've still got your own head on your shoulders. Did you discover when and where that coach will be stopped?'

'About an hour and a half after five o'clock,' he said. 'That's what Boosey reckons. He says poor Mr Bleak the footman's been took particular bad these last days, and got turned off from Myttons on account of Mr Mytton not paying wages for bellyaches; so Boosey'll be on the box himself and they've now had their orders. They're to load a case at Cornhill and leave there by five o'clock; and he reckons it'll take 'em an hour and a half to come to the ford across Rogue's Lane, beyond the plantations by the millpond.'

I digested that in silence before pronouncing, 'Very near exactly as I'd foreseen it all. You perceive here, Maggsy, a remarkable exercise in the Art and Science of Detection. And you're sure you've got that right?'

'That's what Boosey said. He said Jake Tasker and his boys was to be there by six and get themselves well hid, though it would be dark by then and very likely foggy too.'

'You've done very well,' I commended the clever child. 'But was there any more? Did either of 'em say how many men there'd be?'

'Never a word. Only that the gentlemen'd be riding behind the coach but they'd close up on it as it come to the ford. Wasn't much more. Boosey observes he'd best be moving on if he don't want to lose his new job before he draws the profit from it; leaves Tasker cussing and muttering there, something about no more'n a lousy hundred guineas so far as I can hear. Then he finishes his ale too and goes off himself and I start wearing me feet down to the bone again, all the way to West Smithfield this time, a place as bad as Seven Dials, if not worse; Greenhill's Rents, and dead low. He fetches up in what looks like a common lodging house, the kind of place where they give you a bed for a penny and then cut your throat for tuppence; it's the last tenement where the Rents passes into Red Lion Alley if you want him.'

I pondered on that for a time and at last announced, 'No, Master Maggsy. There's little more he could tell me, little more I want to know, save only one thing which will come out at the end; and little more we can do now. I'm persuaded that Mr Dashwood will come to no harm guarded by his two devoted ladies and there's no doubt our merry rogues will go about their stratagems as innocent as kittens. So we'll let our Mr Tasker rest in innocence till Sunday, when we'll have them all in their sins. Tonight we'll take our ease and you shall entertain me with your reminiscences of London life and the doings and observations of Mr William Makepeace the Practical Chimney Sweeper.'

So we supped simply but well enough over an eel pie, a brisket of beef, and various tarts, and then I sat with a pipe or two over my last but one bottle of Madeira while Maggsy related his tales and fables. These I shall not set down here for many were somewhat indelicate, and I myself listened to them with but half an ear while I mused more over the new thought which had come to me. A light that lit up one peculiar circumstance which had perplexed me all along and which, if it were the true illumination, shone like the best wax candle on a particular curious piece of villainy and my own certain reward. With these comforting reflections and my own stratagems for tomorrow devised I at last packed Master Maggsy off to bed, as he was already twitching and snoring like a little hog upon the hearth, and retired to repose myself secure in the continued benevolence of Providence.

After a peaceful night we arose betimes on what were to be the last and most surprising scenes of our curious mystery. These I shall come to quickly, as no doubt by now my publishers will already be counting up on their fingers the cost of paper and printing, which is ever the way of these unhappy people. But there were still certain enquiries to be made, and having breakfasted comfortably I despatched Master Maggsy about some of these, with instructions to ask a few simple questions along the river from Three Crane Stairs by Queen Street to the Waterworks Wharf at London Bridge; thereafter to wait on me by twelve o'clock at the Cornhill Coffee House. Scenting fresh mischief the little rascal went off willingly enough.

By this time it was turning up a fine pretty day, well suited for such travels as I proposed, and true to her word Lady Dorothea's light town carriage was already waiting; a smart turnout, a handsome pair of dapple greys, and a very civil obliging fellow for coachman, together with the message that as I required them there would be this carriage and himself again tomorrow and four other men mounted on horses. In high good humour I had him drive me first to Bow Street; but to set me down and wait for me a discreet distance from the office lest some of those people who are envious of my success should fancy I was getting ideas above my station. Tact and prudence are a nice part of true gentility; besides I did not want my master asking questions.

Happily he was engaged about the business of the court, and I was left to consult with Abel Makepenny, our clerk. Him I desired to inform our master that I had hopes to bring the matter to a conclusion by tomorrow, and promised to show Abel himself as pretty a clutch of villains and as astonishing a story as ever he'd seen by Monday. Then requesting him finally to remind Mr A. about a certain dozen of port promised, if the humour seemed propitious and the gout not too distracting, I turned next to consult that most excellent Plan or Map of London recently engraved for the Phoenix Fire Office by Mr Robert Horwood.

Once again Providence smiled on me, for in a few minutes I discovered the mill pond, the plantations in a wide desolation of marshes, and the ford crossing Rogue's Lane; this coming from Blue Anchor Road and Jamaica Row to Bermondsey, and so on to Tooley Street and London Bridge. In short the route which Mr Mytton's coach must needs follow to come at Greenland Dock; and this, I believe, the first occasion a map of London was ever used for putting down crime. If the time comes when every borough has its own police office and force—whether the public will put up with it or not—some such plan or map should be a part of every equipment.

Still more satisfied I returned to my carriage and now directed my driver to Grub Street, the good fellow plainly taken aback at being ordered to such an address after the pillared and porticoed splendours of Hanover Square, but reassured by my weighty manner. In but a few minutes' more we were setting a spanking pace down the Strand, a sparkling spectacle of shops and establishments with the ladies studying their wares, mail coaches thundering by, street arabs turning cartwheels for ha'pennies, a detachment of the Guards trotting past, young bloods with their phaetons and curricles in a dash and clatter. And my own turnout as smart as the best of 'em.

But arrived in Grub Street Dr Blossum wasn't at first the best pleased to see me, peering ill temperedly at the leaves of a dog-eared old book with a quill poised in his hand; seemingly these scribblers get as broody as old owls, which they much resemble, while about their scratching. To soothe the old gentleman I said, 'Well now, Dr Blossum, I'm grieved to interrupt your learned labours but I've come to take you for a little jaunt. A gossip around the City coffee shops and a ride out as far as Deptford.'

'Can't afford the time,' he declared on a great bellow of snuff, 'got to finish this puff and pigeon's piss for Lady Dorothea, though I doubt the poor distracted soul'll ever read it. All of a flutter, so I hear, over poor Mr Dashwood. 'Twas all over the Lane last night that he's like to die of a mortification before another day's out. Whether you shot the rogue or not, Mr Sturrock, take a pinch of snuff.'

'Let us pray for a good ending,' I said earnestly, at the same time reflecting that the ladies were doing their work excellently well, and adding, 'but I was proposing a jaunt for you and another service to me, Dr Blossum; and did I mention dinner and a dozen or so of oysters on the way?'

'Eh?' he cried, dashing down his quill, 'what's that I heard? Did I hear you say a dozen or so oysters? Well to be sure this is a damnation notioned work and it'll keep, and this tedious wretch Seneca gives a man the gripes. A dinner with a dozen or so oysters is it? Dammit then, what're we standing here for?' he cried, bustling about, getting into his greatcoat and capes, winding a muffler about his throat and clapping a moth eaten beaver upon his head.

So we went on our travels once more, this time towards the Cornhill, Lady Dorothea's coachman now particular wooden faced but remaining civil, and Dr Blossum all agog while I explained what I wanted of him. This namely to pass himself off as a writer on *The London Packet* or *The*

True Briton and peregrinate from one coffee house to another engaging in financial conversation and making certain enquiries. It was a notion which tickled him extravagantly and he wheezed and chuckled and sneezed himself pretty near into an ecstasy; although there was one untoward circumstance in the end. The foolish old man confessed that in his haste and excitement, thinking about those oysters, he had left his purse behind and hadn't so much as a ha'penny piece about him. They are devilish sharp business men, these scribblers, and that cost me half a guinea; it went to my heart, but I reflected that if what I thought now was a true bill it would be returned to me many times more than a hundred fold before all was done.

Arriving safely at Cornhill I dismissed our good charioteer with instructions to rest his horses and himself, even to a quart of ale and victuals if he so desired, and thereafter to meet us again at the Old Swan Tavern by two o'clock; and this also cost me several shillings. Then going our several ways I myself retired to the Cornhill Coffee House once more; still a hive of the industrious ants digging out their gold, the same gentlemen still at their note books, the waiters or servers scurrying from place to place, messengers running in and out.

I shall not weary you with the full tale, but by dint of informing one of the servers privately that I could lay my hands on a thousand or so guineas at present liquid, as the saying is among these curious people, I was very quickly accommodated with a table and several gentlemen all eager to proffer advice and get their fingers in the pie. Thus encouraged it was an easy matter to start the conversation on affairs of the City in general, and bring it about to those of Mytton and Company in particular. So in the pleasantest possible fashion I learned of several curious but not all that surprising matters. First, that Mr Mytton himself, from commonly being one of the most cautious of men, had lately been thought to be taking considerable risks; second,

141

that the house was in shoal water and the loss of any large sum in liquid assets might well be the reef which would sink it; again, that there were several other houses in the City who would not precisely put their own shutters up in mourning should this prove to be the case; and another curious circumstance, that Mytton's office had been closed during the entire business hours yesterday.

Such is City gossip it seems, and well satisfied with these helpful gentlemen I professed myself infinitely obliged for their advice; it should be considered most profoundly, I assured them, and in due course I would call upon them again. Then, receiving several invitations to sup or dine and another to pronounce judgement on an uncommonly fine bottle or two of port, I withdrew most fortunately just as Master Maggsy appeared in the doorway searching for me.

By the look on his wicked face he also had discovered something more, as indeed I had expected he would. 'God's Tripes,' he announced, 'you've done it again. Damned if I know how you bring it off so often, but you're always right. Every one a coconut.'

'If you follow the first principles of detection,' I observed, 'you must of necessity be right. But what in particular this time?'

'A wherry from Dyer's Hall Wharf,' he answered. 'And a hired coach, like you said.'

'Not here, you little chatterbox,' I admonished him. 'There are too many ears about. Let us repair to the Swan Tavern and await Dr Blossum.'

We had no need of that for the good doctor was already waiting for us, his nose twitching like a hound's at the savoury odours, the roaring fire and spits turning, geese, ducks, capons, sirloins, etc., all sizzling and spitting, and an array of pies that he couldn't take his eyes off. 'Well met, Mr Sturrock,' he cried, 'sharp on the minute. And, be-god, they've got as fine a barrel of Whitstables here as ever I've seen. What shall it be? A dozen or so; or two? Eh?'

Cutting short these rhapsodies I said, 'Let's find a bench then and set to,' placing the old guts bag where he could survey the comfortable scene and calling for the oysters to pacify him. Then when his first transports were over, and the better part of the oysters with 'em, I enquired, 'What good did you have?'

'Monstrously gastronomic,' he sighed. 'You're a man after my own heart, Mr Sturrock. Now what was we thinking of eating? And what was that you asked? What good did I have? Well enough. Did you know they call these fellows "underwriters"? And damnation tight lipped for the most part; but there was a deal made right enough, though I could extract little about it.' He sighed once more over the heap of oyster shells and continued hopefully, 'Nonetheless I discovered another as opened his mouth better. He said the premium was uncommon heavy; whatever that means. On account of the French war and privateers, to say nothing of normal sea risks. Couldn't make head nor tail of it myself. He said the premium was fifteen per centum.'

'Fifteen per centum,' I mused. On forty thousand, six thousand pounds; indeed a heavy premium.

'Lord, Mr Sturrock,' the doctor cried in a sudden panic seeing my abstraction, 'you ain't going to let it rest with the oysters, are you?'

'Far from it,' I assured him. 'Take a look for what you fancy now, for we're doing very nicely. I can start to smell our reward, as rich and savoury as that roast sucking pig there.'

He perked up on the instant, echoing, 'Our reward? Did I hear you say "our reward"? God bless me, Mr Sturrock, d'you mean to say you'll push a bit my way?'

'It's early to speak yet,' I told him hastily. 'But I've certain stratagems and we must see how they come out. Let's not spoil a good dinner with business talk, Dr Blossum.'

So we continued like aldermen, the sucking pig and a middling apple pie but with a thought too much cloves in it and last a particular tasty Double Gloucester cheese; the good doctor laying it all away and only pausing occasionally to apostrophize or let fall a philosophical observation. Even Master Maggsy was obliged to cry surrender first, to sit back and watch the old fellow as if adding yet another prodigy to his strange sights, mysteries and wonders of London. But at length I called for the reckoning—damned near giving myself a convulsion of the heart with it—and led them out again on the next part of our odyssey; namely to the ford across Rogue's Lane on Deptford Marshes, for like any good general should I wished to survey our battlefield.

Our good fellow was somewhat astounded at seeing his passengers continually increased, and somewhat more wooden faced when I acquainted him of our destination; but plainly of a better sort than most of these surly rogues —thus proving the superior excellence of Lady Dorothea's establishment, and what a genteel haven for Mr Dashwood —he set off again without a word escaping him. So we turned down to London Bridge, over the river to Tooley Street and so on to the mercantile busyness of Bermondsey; such a wilderness and confusication of timber yards and manufactories, breweries, tanneries and sail makers, rope walks and fell mongers as you ever saw. Dr Blossum was content to doze gently, from time to time letting fall a word or two about oysters and sucking pig, while Maggsy exclaimed at every fresh novelty he observed; but for my part I was concerned merely to stop my nose against a stench of glue, tanning, hides, tar and tallow the like of which had never assailed my nostrils before.

But at last we were out of it to a more rural surrounding, and then a greater desolation. We passed a series of mill leats and the mill pond itself grey under the sky, on to a narrow and twisting road under the dark cover of the plantations and so into the wide emptiness of the marshes; a desolation of brown rushes and waste land with the ford itself another fifty yards further, not all that deep but twenty feet or so wide and enough to slow a coach down. To one side a tangled thicket of scrub and gnarled willow trees, on the other a row of ruined hovels; and yet further on along the flat and empty road, one low solitary building with a thin rag of smoke ascending from its chimney. As I recollected from Mr Horwood's map, that would be the Halfway Inn. A melancholious scene with a light drizzle now falling, the mist rising to meet it, and little more to be seen but the masts and rigging of ships etched against the sky a mile or more away.

Bidding our coachman turn the horses and wait for me on this side of the water I myself ventured further afield on foot, crossing the ford by a rickety plank, surveying the inn from closer quarters, studying the cover, and considering the distances; in general, laying down my tactics. Then returning to the carriage I gave the word for home and set Maggsy to pinching, shaking and bawling the good doctor into wakefulness; a service which he performed with some zest.

This accomplished, and the old gentleman's curses and expostulations stilled, I proceeded to lay before him the whole matter as I now understood it, my stratagems to bring it to a good end, and his own part in the matter, all to the accompaniment of a chorus of ejaculations, exclamations, guffaws, and sneezes. The notion that he was to continue as a writer on *The London Packet* pleased him, as I fancy it tickled his vanity; but he backed like a windy dray horse at the word of fighting and perhaps pistol work. 'No,' he announced, 'I'll not have it. A duel's all very fine when it's but watching other fools kill each other but, God's Weskit, if ever I saw one of them things pointed at me I should piss myself or worse.'

'Dr Blossum,' I retorted, 'you are a necessary part of my

plan; towards the end of our reward. Do you want a new book to write? Or don't you?'

'Books?' he cried. 'Well, the Devil prod you with his fork, you've been roaring on about a book for days. You never stop talking of a damnation book but we don't get any closer.'

'This time I'll engage on it,' I promised. 'And a book on such terms as you never dreamed of before. I wouldn't say but what I might not even bring it to the notice of His Royal Highness the Prince of Wales and make your fame and fortune. Moreover,' I added cunningly, 'do but wait on me at Soho Square in the forenoon tomorrow and we can find time to take a long, late breakfast with nothing stinted before setting out.'

'What's that?' he cried. 'Did I hear you say breakfast? Breakfast is it, eh? Then by God I'm with you. A riotous, cunning rogue you may be, Mr Sturrock, but you've got a very fair understanding of what a man owes to his belly.'

It was concluded on that, and we rattled away home merrily. The dusk was about falling as we reached Cheapside, set Dr Blossum down near enough to Grub Street, and then turned our horses for Soho Square. Here I gave our trusty coachman particular instructions about tomorrow; to have himself and his men and horses present by a little after noon, to bring them well armed with stout cudgels at least, and to come provided with a plenty of ropes. I am a man as likes to have everything to hand. If the good fellow thought anything strange of this he still gave no sign of it, perhaps being naturally sluggish of surprise; but he assured me, wooden faced, of his best attentions as I assured him in return of a handsome reward for himself and his companions.

Thus all now being set in train there was no more to do further than await the event and spend a peaceful evening over my last bottle of Madeira; but not forgetting to look to my pistols.

CHAPTER ELEVEN

So you are to see us now with our forces set out and waiting; not so many as I could have wished for but enough, I
hoped, given tactics and surprise. Dr Blossum had again
consumed such a breakfast that morning as had dumbfounded even me, Lady Dorothea's men had arrived at
Soho Square as appointed, and I had explained our enter-
prise and caused some surprise and merriment by demanding two of them who could make a fair imitation of the
hooting of a melancholy owl. There was a certain purpose
in this, as you shall see. Then with the carriage leading the
way, in which I further instructed Dr Blossum on his part,
and the men following on their horses at a discreet distance
we set off to all appearance a peaceful and harmless cavalcade. In this order we arrived at the mill pond just as the
afternoon's light was starting to fade, for it had turned out
another grey day with a light mist already starting to rise;
again a desolate scene with not a soul in sight on the
deserted landscape.

Here I made my dispositions. The horses were tethered
well inside the trees and our first avian imitator—not without some coarse jesting which shocked me somewhat as
coming from Lady Dorothea's household—concealed by
the mill pond where he could watch the road for a fair
distance back. The other three I settled at the nearer end
of the plantation within sight of the ford, and then took
on Master Maggsy to hide him in the rushes at the other
side of this sluggish stream. Finally I sent the carriage with
Dr Blossum and our driver on as far as the Halfway House

where they might sit in comfort to await their entrance, even over a pot of ale apiece if they chose. Our Dr Blossum, I thought, would look no more than a harmless old traveller there.

The plan was simplicity itself. Our first man watching the road must perceive the lights of the coach when it was still far enough away. Upon which he would let off his owl's cry twice over, and then at once fall back to join his fellows at this end of the plantation. Meanwhile, in case the first call should be too far off for Maggsy to hear it, our second expert here would repeat the cry three times, as it were answering back. On this signal Master Maggsy would then run to the Halfway House, as fast and silently as only a London urchin can, to warn our driver to bring Dr Blossum and his carriage back to the ford.

He would have plenty of time for this as the coach, most likely with a four in hand, would have further to come. So using his judgement he was to bring his carriage to the ford only after the coach itself had arrived there and the battle actually joined; what the academical doctor chose to do at that juncture was his own affair, though I should have need of him later. Our men in the plantation would let the coach and the gentlemen rogues following it pass, and only close in at the rear when we had them all together and I myself gave the signal by discharge of one of my pistols. By this means, I estimated, we should block the road on the far side of the ford, catch the villains about their work red handed, and present ourselves as the intrepid rescuers in a dramatic conclusion.

I found myself a concealment close by the ford in the hollow of an ancient, riven willow tree; and after that there was nothing for it but to wait while the night deepened and a deathlike stillness fell, broken only by the whisper of the dried grasses and a movement of certain small creatures in the wilderness. The mist rose thicker, and with it a weak moonlight, so that all was bathed in a ghostly and insubstantial penumbra. It was a fit occasion for philosophical reflection and moral observations, and I have no doubt I must have composed several, but have now forgotten what they were.

At last there was a movement away in the obscurity of the plantation; the sound of horses and voices muttering together, approaching and resolving into four men in the will-o'-the-wisp light. They stopped by the ruined hovels across the road, dismounted and faded into the blacker darkness there with their animals, one of them cursing softly as he stepped into water, the clatter of hooves, and one of the horses snorting. All was silent again save for the whisper of voices once more and then the snap and flash of a flint as they put light to a candle lantern; and hard on that the cry of an owl faint and far away. It was at once repeated thrice by another close by, and hard on that too another sound from beyond the ford; Master Maggsy's boots scraping on the gravel, the clumsy little wretch.

He was like to have spoiled everything. Two of 'em came out to the road with their lantern, for all the world like a pair of stage comedians looking for a noise in the night. One said, 'There's summat there, beyond the water,' and the other rejoined, 'No more than a sheep or goat; or Polly Knapp's ghost come back to haunt you, Jake.' That would be Master Tasker, I noted. He answered, 'It's a fit place for the old sow, but be damned to your wanchancy talk, Mike Pavitt; 'tis bad luck.' So they stood there listening until the other turned as if to peer towards me, and I caught a clear sight of him in the flickering gleam of the candle; the darkish face, eye patch and black straw hat of the knife throwing little villain Maggsy had described in the Brown Bear. We had a fine catch of herrings ready for the net here.

But they were suspicious, gazing at my concealment, barely a dozen paces away, and I eased my pistols out though praying to Providence that I should not have to use them too soon and so spoil the game. In that fateful moment it all hung on a hair had not the one, Pavitt, cocked up his head like a pointer dog and said, 'Hark!' Clear and distinct in the quietness was the clatter of hooves again, a team by the sound of it, the jingle of harness and the grind of wheels coming fast; and then the first flicker of lamps between the trees.

It was on us before I expected, as big as a ship of the line in the mist; Tasker waving his lantern in front to stop it, the coachman reining in damned near with his leaders in the water and bawling, 'What of hell's this?' and Boosey beside him on the box, another fellow riding guard on the boot behind, and two masked horsemen closing up fast. It was a confusion of trampling hooves, snorting and screams in clouds of steam from the animals; one horseman leaning over to fell the guard with a single cruel blow, the coachman roaring, 'Your pistols, for God's sake, man,' and Boosey dragging these out to strike him treacherously in turn, toppling the poor soul clean off the box and reaching over to snatch up the reins himself. Him I dealt with incontinent, though I wanted the rascal alive if possible. Discharging the first of my armament I aimed at his lower legs; with some happy result judging by the scream that rent the air.

That was very near the end of me for while one rider was already at the coach door, Mr Cullen I fancy, the other by the rear fired back at the flash of my pistol. I heard the ball smack into the tree beside me, and at once returned the like compliment with my second weapon; but missed. A sorry confession and a sorry conclusion. He blazed back and this time took off my beaver; as he might have taken off my head had he aimed an inch or so lower. Plainly this was to be a turbulent affair, no time for niceties, and close quarters the best attack. Cullen then swung round, likewise armed, and he must surely have settled my business but for an act of Divine justice. As the man Tasker roared,

'By God, 'tis Sturrock!' and flung himself on me with his cudgel raised, Mr Cullen fired also and Tasker fell in the way of it to choke off his last word with a scream. So after all his sins the poor villain saved my life; but not willingly.

No historian may ever do justice to battle, there being so many actions, incidents and alarms all at once. Myself now engaging the rascal Pavitt, him coming at me with a knife while Cullen cursed him roundly for another one getting in the way of his second weapon; a voice bawling from within the coach, 'Stop there, we surrender; we surrender I say'; our own carriage now arrived with Dr Blossum leaning out to sneeze and roar encouragement, Maggsy splashing through the water screeching lewd curses and brandishing a fencing post or stave, and my other fellows joining in the fray; two of them falling upon Digby and dragging him from his horse with a rope around his neck. For myself, feeling the knife tear at my coat and losing all patience, I put Pavitt's nose out of joint with a blow from my pistol and further awarded him a thrust in the belly which must near have gutted him; while Maggsy, the jolly little rogue, swung his stave like a Marylebone cricketer and landed Cullen a ringer which laid him senseless against the coach.

It was as good as done with then. We were left the victors, though it was a fearful scene of carnage. Boosey lying in a pool of gore, moaning and clutching a broken knee, Cullen unconscious and Digby half throttled, a taste of things to come; Tasker with not much left of his shoulder and like very soon to pay in full for poor Polly Knapp and Mr Grabble; the little viper Pavitt doubled up and weeping with blood pouring from his flattened snout, and the other two rogues securely held by my own brave fellows. And now Mr Robert Mytton thrusting his head from the coach and demanding, 'What of God's name is this? What is it, I say?' perceiving me and crying, 'Damnation, it's you, Sturrock.'

'It is indeed, sir,' I assured him. 'And a timely intervention if you ask me. These fellows was bent on devilment. It's a good thing we got wind of some mischief and followed 'em. But what are you doing here in this wild and desolate place, Mr Mytton?'

'That's my business,' he retorted.

'Why, no, sir,' I answered mildly enough. 'It looks like robbery on the King's highway; and that's the business of His Majesty.' By this time Dr Blossum was huffing and sneezing at my elbow, ready to play his part as I had instructed him. 'And you, sir?' I enquired, 'if I dare ask, who might you be?'

'Ezekiel Blossum,' he announced, 'sometimes a writer to *The London Packet*, *The True Briton*, *The Times*, and other newsprints. About to visit the Royal Victualling Office and my driver got himself lost on these pestilential marshes. But what's afoot, sir? By God, a desperate affray; saw the entire of it. We'll have an account of this published. Did I hear the name of Mr Mytton?' he asked. 'Of Mytton and Company, bankers?'

'Sir,' Mr Mytton interjected, 'you'll be good enough to mind your own affairs.'

'That accounts for the rumours in the City,' Dr Blossum mused regardless. 'Place is full of rumours. Shipment of gold for the Indies, sailing by the *Nancy Drew* now lying in Greenland Dock.'

'So ho,' I exclaimed, as if a great light had dawned upon my innocence. 'Then that explains it. And explains a deal more besides. I've much to tell you, Mr Mytton; a full explanation of the mystery. So we'd best guard you and your gold as far as the ship, and there you shall hear it.'

'Be damned to you for a puffed up jackass,' he announced. 'I've no time for mysteries. Will you stand aside and let me move on.'

'And this after saving you and your gold?' I asked in reproach, but vowing wickedly that I'd have this haughty banker singing a different tune before another hour or so was out; no man calls me a jackass lightly. I said, 'Moreover it's the mystery of your son, sir,' and added in a tone that admitted no denial, 'there's no help for it. It's a matter of the law now. And your own commission to investigate Mr Robert Mytton's death.'

It was taken with an ill grace, but we ordered our cavalcade, Mytton's coachman being recovered enough to get up on the box again by now. The four lesser rogues we left here in charge of my bold fellows until I could send men from the dockyard to bring them in, and Boosey was helpless, would need a surgeon before he could be moved; but Cullen and Digby were placed in our other carriage, securely trussed, with Maggsy up beside the driver. Dr Blossum and I rode with Mr Mytton, and a somewhat sour and silent journey it was, for he offered not another word to either of us. It was no matter. There would be certain talk with Mr Mytton later on, and much to the point.

In that order we came to the lamps and flares of the dockyard, in a busy confusion of ships and masts and rigging, and after a few minutes more were brought up alongside the *Nancy Drew*; a trim, rakish looking vessel. Here we witnessed a heavy iron bound chest brought from the coach and carried down to the captain's cabin, where we followed ourselves while Mr Mytton offered a tight lipped explanation of who and what we were and our late adventure. There was no great welcome from Captain Hardcastle —as my own sea captain friend had said, like by name as to nature—only four small and grudging glasses of Madeira, and not as good as my own; but after politely begging his permission I at last had our two chief villains brought in.

A very different pair now from the fine gentlemen of Drury Lane. Both with their hands bound behind them and unmasked in their wickedness. Cullen remaining somewhat dazed, bearing the marks of Master Maggsy's

153

dainty handiwork and an uncommonly rich black eye, but Digby still with a certain dark and sardonic humour; and clearly, as I had now thought for several days, the brains of the business.

I told the story plain and clear; starting with Mr Grabble setting the ball rolling with his silly chatter of Mytton and Company's business, the wretched wench who was killed to make room for Nell Ewer in the Mytton household and Nell's part to poison the coach footman with antimony to make way for Boosey. 'She might be the only one who'll escape,' I remarked, 'but we'll have a Hue and Cry out after her.' Then, continuing how Mr Robert Mytton the younger had put two and two together I said, 'I'm surprised he didn't tell you of it, Mr Mytton,' gazing at that iron visaged gentleman damned near as hard as he was watching me.

He did not vouchsafe an answer, and I went on, 'So there you have it. Mr Mytton requested Dashwood to tell Digby that he wished to talk to him "about a legacy"; which Dashwood did next day at rehearsal. Those words sealed Mr Mytton's fate, for Digby knew what they meant and had time to make his preparations. Cullen was to bring the pistol.' I looked at Digby who was listening as if it were some polite tale of a play upon the stage. 'That was Cullen's, Mr Digby, because those pieces by Boutet of Versailles are costly toys for a poor man to possess; and Mr Cullen lives beyond his means.'

The dark rascal did his best to bow to me. 'You think of everything, Mr Sturrock.'

'It's my trade; and your misfortune,' I told him shortly. 'So we come to the fatal night; fatal for you, Mr Digby. You had Boosey take Mr Mytton to the ladies' dressing room knowing that through the Patriotic Spectacle you'd have it clear for twenty minutes or so; moreover you could put it about afterwards that he was there only to meet Miss Virginia Posset. There, while he was expostulating or talking to you and Mr Cullen, Boosey struck him from behind; most likely with a common life preserver.'

There was never a sound in that cabin save the noises from the dockyard, the creak of the ship's rigging and the slap of water at her stern. I continued, 'You, Mr Digby, as being the one named in the message to meet Mr Mytton, went down to the stage wings where you could be observed by all; while Mr Cullen and Boosey waited until that blast of cannon and trumpets and then finished the job off. They at last tipped up the bottle of claret—I fancy that was an afterthought to attract attention—and Mr Cullen took the key from the door and locked it on the outside. All that remained then was to wait until they had enough witnesses gathered before they broke the door down. And no doubt you imagined that my presence was an extra bonus of good luck.'

'Damnation,' Mr Cullen muttered, 'it was more like the Devil's own. For God's sake, how did you tumble to us?'

'Why you damned fool,' I cried, 'by the very trick that was meant to throw me and everybody else off the scent. The locked door. Without that I might have concluded that Mr Mytton was killed by anybody in London; and little hope of ever finding him. A misplaced cleverness for there was only one way it could have been done. Simply that someone of you then present had the key already in his hand; and as soon as the door was burst open with all attention on poor Mr Mytton he thrust it back into the lock on the inside. So from the first I had all my attention on the five people nearest to the door, ruling out poor Polly Knapp; you Mr Digby, and Mr Cullen, Boosey, Mr Jack Dashwood and Lilley.'

'Then why in hell didn't you say so at once and have done with it?' Mr Mytton demanded.

I gazed down at the iron bound box between us. 'Because it was plain there was a deal more hanging on it.'

'Well there it is,' Digby sighed, the cool rogue. 'At least I shall go off to a better audience than we've been getting at Drury Lane of late, for I suppose they'll hang us?'

'With four murders to your credit what d'you expect?' I enquired. 'A chaplet of violets?'

'The curse of it is,' he said, 'we never meant to kill anybody at the start.'

'You won't be the first man to discover he's set something afoot he can't stop,' I observed, and asked, 'Mr Mytton, would you like to have that box opened and show these gentlemen what they're going to hang for?'

If looks might slay he'd have laid me cold as sure as a pistol ball. 'I'll be damned if I will. Get them out of my sight. And yourself with 'em.'

'Well now,' I mused, 'that ain't so easy. For I plan to have 'em sent to Bow Street lock-up this very night if Dr Blossum here'll lend me the favour of his carriage. Which means we must ask you to carry us back to London in yours.'

'And be damned to that likewise,' he announced.

'Come, sir,' I remonstrated, 'that's ungenteel after so much service. And it'll look uncommon poor in the public prints should Dr Blossum here chance to take note of it.'

'By God it will,' that worthy announced, taking a vast pinch of snuff and sneezing fit to blast the ship's timbers. 'Monstrous uncommon poor. *The Packet* can take a particular sharp tone when our editor's a mind to it.'

'Moreover,' I continued, 'I'm not so sure I shouldn't impound that box as being material evidence in highway robbery and murder. Not that I'd wish to cause inconvenience,' I added. 'And no doubt Captain Hardcastle wants to make his ship ready for sea.' I observed the look which passed between those two hard faced men, one of iron and the other oak, and finished, 'I could explain to my master, the Bow Street magistrate, that I saw fit to let the box go, being offered every other assistance by Mr Mytton. Or on the other hand I can say that I deemed it wise to have the contents examined.'

There was another hard silence until the captain advised, 'You'd best do as the fellow asks, Mr Mytton. I've all your documents of lading here completed, and it's a simple matter after all.'

I was not so sure it was myself but did not remark on that, and after a few more tight lipped words exchanged and certain papers being signed by the captain and handed to Mr Mytton he issued a curt invitation to join him in his coach. Our commoner prisoners by now brought to the dockyard to be lodged overnight until I could arrange a delivery to Bow Street, we set off once more for our triumphal return through the mists and desolation of the marshes on the four or five miles to London. A majestic procession with two horsemen riding ahead, next Lady Dorothea's carriage bearing Cullen and Digby to their well deserved judgement and Maggsy with the driver on the box, then the good doctor and myself with Mr Mytton in his coach, and two more riders in the rear.

For some little time it was a silent ride, Mr Mytton seemingly lost in his own reflections, until I coughed as humbly as one of his clerks and said, 'I hope we can look for some commendation, sir.'

'You're a damned insolent rascal,' he retorted, 'and I shall go to the trouble of writing a memorandum to your superiors to say so.'

I gave Dr Blossum a nudge to remind him of his part, and he remarked, 'It's a poor return for saving your gold, sir. In general the reward for stolen property is ten per centum of the value. Begod,' he said, '*The Packet*'s going to be devilish sharp about this; and what *The Times* might say I hardly dare to think. But I'd express an opinion that it won't do the House of Mytton a lot of good.'

'A pox on your *London Packet* and *The Times*,' cried Mr

Mytton rudely. 'And on you too. There was no stolen property.'

'Why no, sir,' I agreed. 'And none to be stolen neither. Not unless you count a few bars of lead, or whatever you put in that box for weight.' As once before I was concerned to see what kind of seizure Mr Mytton would take, but foiled of it this time by the darkness; nevertheless there was a stricken silence. I went on, 'The real shipment of gold, Mr Mytton, was conveyed in secret by you to the *Nancy Drew* from Dyer's Hall Wharf on Friday last. Whether that shipment was privately insured elsewhere I neither know nor care. What I do know is that the box you carried today was underwritten in the value of forty thousand pounds against a premium of six thousand. In short, sir, you knew of and expected an attempt on that cargo and made your dispositions accordingly. Let that box be carried off, and you stood to gain a clear four and thirty thousand.'

'What's this I hear?' Dr Blossum demanded. 'What's this, eh? An insurance take on?'

'As pretty as you've ever seen,' I told him. 'And, come to think of it, the first I've ever heard of myself.'

'You're a fool,' Mr Mytton answered. 'And, by God, I'll see you broke for this. Would I have travelled with that box myself if I had known it was to be attacked?'

'You had to. Had you sent some mere clerk or groom the underwriters might've started asking questions. And you're no coward; I'll say that for you,' I continued remorselessly, 'Whether you had some inkling of a plot arising from Mr Grabble's foolish chatter, or whether your son told you of it I don't know. You was at loggerheads over Lady Dorothea and he might not; but I think he did. And when I brought you that letter from the lady you was of two minds whether to tell me to go to the devil or let me investigate. You concluded on the investigation, as if you stopped it and then the robbery took place there might

158

have been some ugly questions raised again; but you had your own suspicions about the young gentleman's death. In plain, you was pulled both ways, Mr Mytton. Well,' I concluded, 'he was dead and nothing you could do would bring him back again. No doubt you were wise by your own lights to make what you could out of it.'

It was hard to tell whether Mr Mytton's voice was choked with rage or by the various stenches of Bermondsey through which we were now passing. He just got out, 'What do you want?'

Now will you believe this? That after so much work and expense myself I was of a sudden sick to the belly and desired no more of it; I had all the villains I wanted and that was enough. I said, 'For my part be damned to you. But I'll take twenty-five guineas apiece for these brave fellows who came out with us tonight. And I'd advise Dr Blossum he must make his own agreement. But very likely there's a book of some sort he'd like to write.'

'And begod there is,' the doctor cried. 'Next to putting a full account of this in *The London Packet* there's nothing I'd like better. Listen now, sir,' he begged. 'How does this take your fancy? "Observations on our Present Banking Systems and how they increase the Wealth of Nations. By Ezekiel Blossum, M.A., Ph.D., and inscribed to that Patron of the Arts and Master of Finance, Robert Mytton Esq."'

That brought a long silence while we rattled into Tooley Street, coming up to London Bridge, a few lights and torches now passing us outside. Then Mr Mytton spoke. 'I'll give a hundred guineas.'

'What?' Dr Blossum wailed. 'What's that you say? Dammit, you'll starve me. It'll take a year or more to write.'

Defeated as Mr Mytton might be, the banker was still uppermost. 'Two hundred; but not a penny more.'

'You'll give five hundred,' I said with no further nonsense. 'And we'll have an attorney at law to draw up the contract.'

So that also was concluded, and we parted with Mr Mytton at Bow Street; and in no very pretty temper. There I attended to certain formalities on the delivery of my two precious rogues, the others to be collected from Greenland Dock on the morrow. This settled we repaired to supper at Mr Hackett's eating house, where Master Maggsy rehearsed his recollections of the Great Battle, I composed several moral observations on villainy and bankers, etc., and Dr Blossum finished by falling into my arms and weeping with joy. A most untoward circumstance; you should always be careful how you do these damned scribblers a kindness for they know neither restraint nor gentility.

There is little more to relate. I grieve that Nell Ewer escaped, but I'll have her yet; and I shall draw a kindly veil over the fate of our other rogues. Holy Moses came creeping back to Seven Dials in time, and I forgave the canonical old rascal his small part of the business as I still have use for him in Maggsy's education; Dr Blossum, I consider, being apt to put ideas into the child's mind. For the rest Lady Dorothea duly presented her doting father with a fine bouncing grandson and, as I prognosticated, Mr Dashwood entered Parliament; a fit place for him. Also Mrs Huxey from time to time sends me an affectionate billet doux.

And so I subscribe myself once more, your humble and obnt servant to command, Jeremy Sturrock.